GIVE ME ONE NIGHT

McLaughlin Brothers 4

JENNIFER ASHLEY

JA / AG Publishing

Chapter One

Ryan

I CAN'T BELIEVE you're breaking up with me!"

That's my nine-year-old self, bellowing my agony at nine-year-old Calandra, my girlfriend, my soul-mate, my life.

She gazes at me sorrowfully, her dark brown hair in pigtail braids that I thought the coolest style ever. "I'm sorry, Ryan. I just need time."

"Time for what?" My heart hurts so bad I want to rip it out of my chest. "I asked you to *marry* me. I thought you loved me."

"I do love you." Calandra reaches a small finger to my cheek. "It's you and me. Always. But I'm not ready for that kind of commitment. I just need ..." She huffs a breath and swings her arms. "To figure things out."

"But I *love* you! I don't understand what the problem is."

"It's ..." She shrugs, stuffing her hands into her jeans pockets. "It's complicated. I need to be alone a little bit. To get to know me."

"Oh. Sure. Right." I slam my arms over my chest. "To find yourself."

"Exactly." Calandra eyes me critically. "Wouldn't hurt you to do that too."

"Yes, it would. Calandra, don't do this."

I'm supposed to be cool, not caring that the woman of my dreams is stomping on my heart. Chicks are a dime a dozen, right? That's what Austin says, and he's only five years old.

"Ryan." Calandra shakes her head. She has wise eyes for one so young. She leans to me—she's taller than me at that time in our lives—kisses me lightly on the lips, turns, and walks away.

"Calandra!" I shout after her.

I ball my fists and make myself keep my feet still. I will not, *will not*, run after her across the school ground like a big loser. The fight to stay put is tough, but I do it.

She looks back at me one more time. The expression on her face holds pain, as much as I feel. She gives me a little wave, then turns around and heads back into the school building.

Gone.

That was the first time Calandra and I broke up,

and it was a kick in the gut. I'd been so arrogant, thinking I'd propose and we'd be engaged—you know, for the next twenty or so years. The wedding date was comfortably in the vague future.

I'd gone and blown it. Before lunch, Calandra and I had been inseparable. After lunch, I'd been stupid enough to think she'd be mine forever.

Even my dad's fabulous sour cream chocolate cake couldn't make me feel better. He's the baker in our family. His words of wisdom did help, though. He advised me to wait, let Calandra have some time, and see what happened.

Six months later, after a chance encounter at a waterslide park, Calandra and I have a huge, long argument, clear the air, and end up back together. Just like Dad predicted. He's a smart man.

Calandra and I are together for the next couple years, breaking up again when we're thirteen. My hormones start to rage by then, and I stupidly suggest maybe we should try to see other people. Where I'd thought I'd meet these other girls when I was thirteen and hadn't had my growth spurt yet, I don't know, but the words came out.

Calandra doesn't want to break up then, but she kisses me softly, says good-bye, and walks away, giving me plenty of time to regret opening my big, stupid mouth.

On the first day of high school for both of us, we run into each other, laugh at our silly, young selves of eight months before, talk, share a lunch table, and by that evening, are back together again.

High school is a time of rapid change, with me finally growing taller than Calandra, and Calandra filling out in a fascinating and very distracting way— you can trace Calandra's change from girl to woman by my plunging grade-point average.

We break up and make up at least twice a year, and as we do, we grow closer and closer. My family loves her, and anything I do with my brothers, Calandra is included. Zach, Ben, or Austin will say, "Where's Calandra?" Or "Isn't she coming?" in puzzlement if I go anywhere with them alone. She's been their honorary sister since grade school.

Next is college. We continue our break-up, make-up pattern while we both suffer the September heat at Arizona State's main campus, and then enjoy the mild winter months lounging outside to study or kiss. We'll be incredibly loving, and then have arguments of spectacular magnitude. Calandra usually wins the arguments, but making up with her afterward is seriously worth it.

Our relationship has gone physical by then, and most nights sees me in Calandra's bed, or she in mine— whoever's roommate is out. Only dire emergency keeps me away, and it has to be really dire.

After we graduate, she cum laude, I start working at my mom and dad's business, McLaughlin Renovations. Calandra lands a job as a writer and editor at a local magazine. She loves getting to know her city and the people in it, she says.

We continue to see each other as often as work lets us, and spend our weekends together. We both love to hike, and our campouts in Arizona's mountains and back country are memories we'll treasure. The breaking up portion of our relationship has ceased as we realize that there's no one else for either of us.

Our families wonder when we're going to tie the knot, and for the next few years, they ram some not-so-subtle hints at us. But Calandra and I have a good thing going, and we're not in a hurry to make our relationship satisfy anyone but ourselves.

But I have plans. I wait until we're both settled in our careers, no longer kids, and ready for the next phase of our lives.

One balmy Valentine's Day, when we're both heading for the end of our twenties, I take Calandra to our favorite restaurant, order our favorite wine, and clear my throat.

I slide a small box from my pocket, pretending my hands aren't shaking like hell. I leave my chair, and in front of God and everybody in the restaurant, I kneel next to her and hold out the box.

"Calandra Stevenson," I say. "I've known you since we were knee-high to a grasshopper, as my dad says. We've been through thick and thin, up and down, and ..."

Calandra stares at me, stunned, tears filling her big

brown eyes. My carefully rehearsed speech goes out of my head—to hell with it.

"You are so beautiful," I stammer. "Will you marry me?"

I flash back to that day when we were nine, when she'd gazed at me sorrowfully and told me she needed time.

Tonight, Calandra's eyes continue to fill, tears spilling to her cheeks.

"Ryan," she whispers. "Do you even have to ask? *Yes*."

She launches herself at me, and I catch her in my arms while the restaurant goes wild with cheers.

I take Calandra to my parents' house, where my brothers and folks wait, and we celebrate with champagne and gladness.

Calandra and I celebrate again later at my house. She's always sweet in public, but in bed, Calandra is a firecracker. We make love far into the night, both of us crying our passion, laughing, coming, collapsing.

I hold her that night, the happiest man in the world.

Too bad about all the shit that rains down after that.

Chapter Two

Ryan

THE TROUBLE STARTS the following Monday. I work a long day and go to bed early, Calandra spending time with her family that night.

At two in the morning, my phone wakes me. It's Calandra, so I answer it. Anyone else and I'd have thrown it across the room.

"Wha ...?" I mumble.

"Hey, Ryan, you asleep?" Calandra's voice is chipper, upbeat, way too energetic, and a little bit slurred. The family party must have included wine.

"Yep. Sound asleep. I'm coming to you in a dream. What's up?"

"How do you feel about Hawaiian?"

I pause, not sure I've heard right. "Hawaiian what?"

"As a theme. For our wedding."

"Hunh?" I haven't even considered a theme—we're supposed to have a theme? "You mean like leis and grass skirts?"

Calandra bursts out laughing. "That's Hollywood Hawaiian, and totally wrong. I mean real Hawaiian, like making our backyard pool into a beach scene and serving Hawaiian food and drink. Like pog."

I have to be dreaming. I snap on the light, check the bedside clock. Nope, it's two a.m., and my fiancée is calling me to yammer about Hawaiian-themed weddings.

"Like *what*?"

"Pog. It's wonderful—passion fruit, orange, and guava juice mixed together."

"Sweetie, you are drunk, and I am wiped. I love you, baby. Good night."

"Wait ..." Her wail pulls me back. "You can't go yet. We make all these decisions together, right? Anyway, it's not my idea. It's my cousins'. Candy and Mandy."

"Candy and—?"

"Candy and Mandy. The twins. You remember. They have that cabin in Pinetop. It's not their real names. It's Candace and Mary. But they've always been Candy and Mandy."

"I am dreaming this, I swear to God."

"They want to help plan the wedding. Do you think it's a great idea?"

I drag in a breath, taking in cool, dry spring air. "If you called to ask my opinion, here it is: We don't do a theme. We have you and me and our family in a simple service." When Calandra says nothing, I soldier on. "As long as I'm marrying you, baby, I don't need all that other stuff."

More silence. As it stretches I have the feeling I've just said The Wrong Thing.

"Calandra?" I ask hesitantly.

"Never mind." Her voice is bright, too high. "Good night, Ryan."

Click.

I stare at the phone which briefly says, *Call Ended*, before it winks out. I toss the phone to the other side of the bed, fall back onto the mattress, and cover my eyes with my arm.

"*Shit.*"

———

Calandra

I face Ryan Tuesday at lunch, the day after my drinking spree with my cousins and friends. Ryan's family's business isn't too far from where I work at the local magazine on Missouri, and this is our favorite sandwich shop.

"Sorry." I rub my temples as an iced tea lands on the table in front of me. I seize it and take a deep gulp, my mouth parched. "I kinda overdid it last night."

"With wine?" Ryan keeps his voice soft, but it's still too loud for my hungover brain. His blue eyes hold wariness, but those beautiful eyes are all that are keeping me calm right now.

"Tequila shots. We had a contest." I rub my temples again, stifling a groan.

"Did you win?" Ryan asks in amusement.

"I don't know."

Ryan reaches across the table and encloses one of my hands in his. He has large, strong hands, always gentled for me. I used to be taller than this handsome man, who now tops me by a foot. He's filled out with athletic grace and honed muscles, which I touch as much as possible when we're in bed.

"Sounds like you *did* win," he says. "Better luck next time." He chuckles at his joke.

"Things are a little hazy. Sorry I woke you."

"I don't mind my sweet honey calling me in the middle of the night. But maybe next time we can have some sexy talk instead of you telling me I have to wear a grass skirt to my own wedding."

I grope through the fog of my memories to figure out what he's talking about. "I nixed the faux-Hawaiian idea."

Ryan lets out a breath of relief. "Thank you." He squeezes my hand. "Sorry I pissed you off about that. I was half asleep. Not thinking."

"That's not why I was mad—I don't think. This wedding has to be good. My parents have been going on at us for years about when you and I are going to make it official. So we have to do more than stand up with a minister in front of our families. They want a show."

"Mmm." Ryan's mirth fades. "My family is kind of bugging me about the same thing."

"So when you said we didn't need to do anything special, I thought you weren't taking it seriously enough." I gaze at him with my aching eyes, hoping he'll understand.

"Of course I'm taking it seriously, sweetheart." Ryan leans closer. "I want to marry you. I want to wake up next to you for the rest of my life. But I want the wedding to be about *us*, not them."

I have to laugh. "Where have you been? Weddings are always about the guests and the family. The bride and groom endure it to make everyone happy. Otherwise everyone would have a quick read-through with a judge or priest and save a lot of trouble."

"People *do* do that. They go to Las Vegas. Or the courthouse. Easy."

"If it were just the two of us in the equation, I'd be all for it." I sigh, gripping his hands. "But my family is so excited. They want to help, and I don't have the heart to tell them no. Planning a wedding is tough anyway. I could use the assistance."

"Okay." Ryan withdraws his hand to pick up his

iced tea and down half of it. He crunches one of the ice cubes. "I get it. Big ceremony. Dance the Charleston at the 20s-themed reception. Whatever. As long as you and I end up together by the time we escape the crowd, I'm fine."

"Are you?" I study him—I've known this man all my life, but he can still surprise me. "'Cause that would be a load off my mind."

"Sure." Ryan shrugs, too casually. "I was kidding about the 20s theme, so don't get that gleam in your eyes."

"I don't have a gleam. Though it's not a bad idea. Easy costumes—suits and short dresses."

Ryan groans. "I get what you're saying—the wedding is for everyone but us—but won't they be happy if you're in white lace, I'm in a tux, and there's flowers and cake?"

"Yes ..." I agree. My cousins, both sweet girls, had come up with crazier and crazier ideas last night. I knew they'd finally latch onto one of them and run, because that's what they did.

"I hear a *but* in your voice," Ryan rumbles. "Next thing I know, you're going to ask for something impossible, like my brothers behaving themselves."

I grin. "Impossible? Ben can be so sweet."

"I wasn't talking about Ben. I was talking about Zach and Austin, the dreaded duo."

I give him a patient look. "I know your brothers. Have for decades. Zach and Austin rarely hang out together. They're too similar, and they clash. It's Ben and Zach, you and Austin."

"Not in this case. They have wedding fever, those two dudes. Ben wisely backs away and runs when they start up."

"This I have to see." I poke at my iced tea with my straw. "I'm glad your brothers are on board, though. Mom wants to have a big get-together this Saturday night, your family and mine, to discuss the wedding."

Ryan glances up from taking a drink, with a rabbit-in-the-headlights stare. "Really?"

"Yes, really. And before you decide you have a sudden, urgent business meeting in Kingman ... " I hold his gaze, and Ryan flushes. "Let me put it this way. *I* have to go, and I am *not* putting up with constant questions all night long about where you are. Please don't do that to me, Ryan."

"Would I?" He's so innocent.

"Not intentionally, but that's what will happen. Please save me from the torture."

Ryan makes a noise of exasperation. "Fine. I'll be there. But we will get one thing straight from the start. This is *our* wedding. I'm okay with making our families happy, but when everything boils down, it's ours. I'm going to insist."

"Sounds good to me." I take his hand, and we share a long look that has nothing to do with family or weddings or drunk phone calls in the middle of the night.

It's Ryan and me, the special bond we've always shared stretching between us. I see it in his eyes, the deep love, the history we've experienced. Even when we're furious with each other, that bond is still there.

I feel it between us as we clasp hands across the table, and I know it will always be there. Ryan is right—it's him and me, and nothing else matters.

———

Ryan

"Enjoy your freedom now, bro," my brother Austin says to me. We're at Calandra's parents' home in Arcadia that Saturday evening, a sprawl of a house on a sprawl of land, the kind of property that's getting rare around here. It's evening, the sun slipping away into the coolness of a desert spring night, but it's warm enough to cook out. Barbecues are going on the lawn, my dad and Calandra's grilling enough meat to feed a parade.

I sip beer in the back yard with my three brothers, while Calandra and her friends and cousins celebrate on the patio.

"What are you talking about?" I ask Austin.

"Yeah, Ryan's never had any freedom," Zach says. "He's been with Calandra since he was yay high." He flattens his hand alongside his thigh to illustrate.

"It's overrated." Ben drinks from his bottle of craft beer. "The freedom of the single life."

Ben's the family nerd, and while he's had girl-friends here and there, he's not what you'd call a party animal. He's more at home with computers, online gaming, and reading.

"True," Zach agrees. Zach, two years younger than me and closest to my age, had a bad breakup a couple years ago, and he's melancholy. I know he doesn't miss his girlfriend all that much—it wasn't the best relation-ship—but he's lonely and feels it.

Austin stares at Ben and Zach in amazement. "Are you kidding me? This town is great for single guys. Go to a club once in a while; hell, even a sports bar, and enjoy yourselves."

"Different woman every night," I say to my youngest brother, shaking my head. "How do you keep track?"

Austin rolls his eyes. He's handsome, knows how to dress well, and drives a sleek sports car. "I don't have a different woman every night."

"He has a spreadsheet," Ben says, straight-faced. "He's trying to make me create a database for him."

Austin growls and takes a mock swing at Ben, who dances back, wearing a quiet grin. Zach steps forward to defend Ben, and Austin rolls his eyes again. "What-ever." He walks away, heading for the cluster of women on the patio.

"He's always looking for his dream girl," Zach says as we watch Austin saunter toward the ladies.

"He had one," Ben reminds us. "Brooke."

"Yep. And he'll have to deal with her, because she'll be one of Calandra's bridesmaids." I send Zach a pointed look. "So will Abby Warren."

Zach has been staring off into the distance as though calculating how much time he has to politely stay before he's out of here, but at the name, he snaps his attention back to me.

"Abby Warren?"

"The very one. You used to have a thing for her, right?"

Zach's forehead wrinkles. "That was like a hundred years ago. I haven't seen her in ages. Hunh."

I exchange a look with Ben, who gives me one of his slow smiles. It's good to see Zach interested. He let the breakup hit him too hard.

I take a thoughtful sip of beer. "Help me survive this wedding mania, all right? Things are getting out of hand."

I expect my brothers to have my back or at least cheer me up about wedding craziness, but Zach only claps me on the shoulder. "Suck it up, bro. Nothing's too good for Calandra, right?"

"Right," I say hesitantly.

"It'll be a breeze," Zach says. "Stop whining. Let's go get some eats. I'm starving."

"What's new?" Ben asks. They stride across the

darkness toward the barbecues, like primitive man drawn by fire.

I can go with them and talk about cuts of meat like the masculine dudes we are, or I can join the ladies. Ladies it is. They smell better, and Austin, who's already flirting his ass off, needs a keeper.

I approach the patio, which is a long, large tiled area with glass doors leading to a living room, a family room, the kitchen, and way down the row, the master bedroom. The Stevensons have furnished the patio with outdoor sofas and chairs, a clay fire pit for cold nights, misters for hot ones. Right now the fire pit is flickering, and a soft breeze wafts across the space, bringing feminine voices with it.

As soon as I step out of the dark and under the lights, all chatter ceases. Faces turn to me, gracefully curved bodies pausing as the ladies take me in. I feel like a juicy sirloin my soon-to-be pop-in-law is assessing for the grill. Austin stands behind them exuding glee.

Calandra, the love of my life, my partner and help-meet, the woman who will be at my side forever, grins at me.

"What do you think?" she asks her girlfriends and cousins—the two who look exactly alike are Candy and Mandy. "Can you see Ryan in a sarong? He has the legs for it."

Chapter Three

Ryan

I CAN'T STOP myself looking down at my legs bared from the knee in my canvas shorts. The ladies shriek with laughter.

"Is this the Hawaiian idea again?" I growl.

"No, we've dropped that," Calandra says. "We've moved on to a more general tropical beach theme."

"In Arizona?"

"Why not? It's going to be warm, why not go for it?"

Candy, or Mandy, breaks in. "Calandra will be in a sarong too."

That I can get into. My mind floats to a picture of Calandra walking toward me in a bikini top, a flowing, colorful sarong around her waist. She'll stroll casually, cloth-enhanced hips swaying. She'll reach out to brush my arm, then she'll go on by, untying the bikini top as she passes.

"Okaaayyy." I draw out the word.

I must look like a gobsmacked idiot, because the women and Austin burst out laughing.

"One vote for tropical beach theme," Mandy or Candy says.

"He's not thinking about the wedding," Austin adds confidently.

More laughter, because he's right. Austin sends me a grin like the shit he is.

I want to cut Calandra out of the crowd and talk to her alone, but that's not going to happen. She's surrounded by friends and family. I'm the groom-to-be, so I'm the butt of their jokes right now.

That's fine. The sparkle in Calandra's eyes and the glow on her face are worth it.

————

I HOPE THAT BY THE TIME THE COOKS HAVE finished, and we're all stuffing our faces, the wedding talk will be over, but no such luck. My brothers encourage the conversation, and the tropical beach theme resurfaces. The guests will have hibiscus flowers in their hair, and sarongs will be the thing.

I know everyone's joking, but I don't like the contemplative interest on my mother's face. She's queen of organization, and if she decides her oldest son should step to the altar in a piece of flowered cotton and nothing else, it could happen. I look to my dad for help, but he sits and smiles, as usual, letting my mom take an idea and run with it.

As more and more beer is passed around, the plans get wilder. I laugh, showing I'm a good sport, even when Austin suggests we do a circus theme and take our vows on a trapeze. Calandra throws a roll at him, which he deftly catches.

The night goes on, and I realize, by the end of it, that I've lost all control of the situation. Not to mention my wedding, and by extension, my own life.

I decide to talk to Calandra when I volunteer to help with the dishes. I figure everyone else will flee when it's time to do the grunt work of clearing the table, but it isn't to be. As soon as I hop up to carry out my dishes, everyone else does as well.

"Can we talk?" I ask Calandra as she rushes past me, hands full of plates.

"Little busy right now." She flashes me a smile, but doesn't slow down.

I follow her. "Later tonight?"

"My cousins are spending the night. Girl time."

She hurries into the busy kitchen, me right behind her. "Tomorrow? Lunch?" I persist.

"Meeting with my bridesmaids. Haven't seen Brooke or Abby in a while, so it will be a long after-noon. Monday after work?" Her voice lowers seductively, and I want to throw the plates against the wall and haul her down the hall to her old bedroom.

I deflate. "Can't. Dad and I are taking clients to their new house. Promise made a long time ago."

"That's important." Calandra wrinkles her nose at me. "We'll have other times to talk."

When? I wonder. "Right. I'll call you tomorrow night."

"Don't be mad." Calandra flashes her beautiful smile at me. "This will all come out okay."

She's right. I'm marrying the woman I love more than my own life. All this frenzy will fade.

Austin strides by, deep in an argument with Candy (or Mandy), about what color football jerseys the groomsmen should wear.

Calandra bursts out laughing and turns away. The sound of her laughter brings home what a lucky shit I am, and my frustration dissolves on a warm wave of love.

Calandra

I HAVEN'T SEEN ABBY OR BROOKE IN WHAT SEEMS like forever, and on Sunday at lunch we do the high-pitched squee women do when they're excited by meeting their friends. The more we love them, the more piercing the shriek.

We about break the windows with it in a cute restaurant on Seventh Street. I hug Abby, who's a bit shorter than I am and plump in the right places, her dark hair tucked into a neat bun.

Brooke is tall and willowy, like a fashion model, her black hair sleek down her back, her dark skin setting off her beautiful blue dress.

"You two are gorgeous," I say. "And, wow, you let me hang out with you."

We hug again then we finally settle down, Brooke waving her hand to order wine. Abby and I let her make the choice, because Brooke knows all about wine.

"Ring. Ring. Let's see the ring." Abby happily reaches for my hand which I flutter in her direction.

"Nice," Brooke says approvingly as they study the round-cut diamond on the gold band. "Elegant. Ryan gets a gold star."

I retrieve my hand but rest it on the table so the ring is visible. "Once, when Ryan and I were shopping a long time ago, one like this caught my eye in a jewelry store window. Stopped me in my tracks. I raved about it. We were fourteen. He remembered."

My friends lean into each other and say, "Awwww."

"Another gold star for Ryan." Abby lifts her hand to high-five me.

The waiter arrives with our wine, and we spend a moment sipping and making appreciative noises. It's a red, robust but not sour.

"The McLaughlin brothers can be sweet," Brooke concedes, her glass dangling from her fingers. "When they want to be."

Abby and I send Brooke a sympathetic glance. "Sometimes it doesn't work out," I say.

Brooke and Austin had been an item once, a few years ago. They'd been good together, both loving fine wine and great cars—Brooke is part owner of a luxury car dealership now. They'd broken up, big time. Brooke is still sensitive on the subject.

"Speaking of sweet," Abby says. "I have an important question." She leans forward, her brown eyes impish. "Is Zach still cute?"

Brooke splutters with laughter, her discomfort gone. "You remember him?"

"Of course I remember him. He was my first kiss." Abby blushes. "A long, long, long, long time ago. I moved away right when things were heating up. Ah, well. Memories."

I fold my arms on the table. "I'm biased, because I think Ryan's the best looking McLaughlin, but I can tell you with some authority that yes, Zach is still cute."

"As a button," Brooke adds.

"For whatever reason buttons are cute," Abby says. "Don't either of you dare tell him I asked that. He probably doesn't remember me at all."

"Mmm, I wouldn't say that," I muse. "But you'll find out soon enough. You're my maid of honor, and Zach's Ryan's best man."

"Cool." Abby brightens. "We'll be a couple again. Briefly."

Brooke sends me a dark look. "As long as you don't pair me with Austin."

"Of course not." I reach across the table and pat her hand reassuringly. "You'll be with Ben."

"Okay, that I can handle. Ben's a sweetheart." Her eyes narrow. "Who's with Austin?"

"Ryan's Great Aunt Mary. She's looking forward to it."

Brooke relaxes into a smile. "Good for Aunt Mary. I love her."

"So does Austin, so he'll behave. Mostly." I watch my friends enjoy picturing the pairing of Ryan's great aunt, who is by no means feeble, with the lady's man Austin, then my shoulders sag. "I'm afraid Ryan wants to bail though. Wedding planning is already getting too much for him."

"Guys aren't into weddings like we are," Abby says quickly. "This is our moment, when we get to put on a magnificent dress and say, *Look at me, world! I'm beautiful, I'm marrying this lucky guy, and the rest of you can suck it.*"

I laugh, but Brooke shakes her head. "It's more like *I'm going into bondage for the rest of my life, so I need this big party as a sendoff.*"

"That's cynical." I take a deep drink of wine.

"Wedding traditions are all about women giving up their lives for their mates," Brooke tells me. "The white dress to say she's pure, even though *he* doesn't have to be, the wedding bands stand in for shackles, *and* until —say, fifty years ago?—a woman had to promise to obey her husband, no matter what."

"Thanks a lot." I give her a stern look. "Whatever happened to marriage being about joining in love and partnership? Facing the ups and downs of life together?"

Brooke and Abby exchange a serious glance then dissolve into laughter. "Your face," Abby chokes out.

"It's your wedding, honey," Brooke says. "It's all about what you say it is."

"It will be beautiful," Abby promises. "April is a good month for it. Warm enough for an outdoor reception but not so hot we all melt. Plus, it rarely rains in April. Very practical."

"Where's it going to be?" Brooke breaks in.

"A church on Central we both love," I tell them, my enthusiasm returning. "We've been going there off and on for years, whenever we can pry ourselves out of bed on Sunday morning."

"I can get you the cathedral." Brooke takes on her efficient-planner demeanor. "You're Episcopalian, right? I know a guy who's friends with the bishop and his wife. I sold him a Ferrari. The guy, not the bishop. If you want the cathedral, I can set it up."

"It might be a bit large for what we need," I begin.

"It's not that big, as far as cathedrals go," Brooke assures me. "But it's nice, and will be awe-inspiring.

Good photo ops. I know a decent photographer. He does celebrity weddings—excellent photos but he's not intrusive. No climbing over the altar to shove a camera in your face."

"We were going to have everyone take their own pics and send them to us," I say faintly.

Brooke and Abby glance at each other again. Clearly I'm a sad case who doesn't know how to plan her own wedding and need their help. I take another hasty sip of wine.

"You won't regret a professional photographer," Brooke says. "Besides, how else will you have a photo of Ryan's face when he sees you in your tutu?"

I nearly spew my wine across the table. I swallow and cough. "My what?"

The two of them go off in laughter, falling into each other. I wait patiently until they're done.

"No tutus," I say firmly. "Or beach themes, or sports themes, or anything like that. A simple cere-mony. That's all I want. We want."

"Of course, honey." Brooke makes herself calm down, but her smile is wide. "No crazy themes. A wedding dress, the cathedral, photographer, flowers, the guys in tuxes, Abby, me, and Great Aunt Mary in the traditional bridesmaid color coordination, a recep-tion spread with a band, a tent, and lots of great food. All you need. And invitations, based on your colors. What colors are you doing?"

"I don't know yet."

Abby stares at me. "Yet? You only have a few months. Unless you mean April a year from now."

"No. This April. Ryan and I have been together for what, twenty years? We don't want to wait any longer."

"Then we have to get in front of this," Brooke says, and Abby nods. "But don't worry. We're on it. Abby and I will divide up the chores and work with your mom to get this all done. You sit and admire your ring."

"But ..." I feel all control of my special day slipping from my grasp.

"And warm up for the wedding night with Ryan," Abby says. "You need to rehearse exactly what you're going to do. Over and over. Leave the boring stuff to us."

"It's not boring," I try to explain.

I'm talking to the air. Abby pulls out a small laptop —she's carrying a laptop to Sunday lunch—and she and Brooke start making notes.

I think about confessing to Ryan that while the silly wedding ideas have been tabled, the bulk of the planning was just ripped out of my hands. I picture his annoyance, which probably will match mine.

I try to wrest control away once more, but Abby and Brooke have their heads together, coming up with more and more things to add, like the music at the wedding, decorating the pews with flowers, scattering the aisle with rose petals, and what kind of champagne to serve. The best, Brooke says. She knows a woman at a vintners who can give us a deal.

I can only sit back, sip my wine, and try to figure out how to explain this to Ryan.

———

Ryan

SEVERAL WEEKS GO BY WITHOUT ME ONCE SEEING Calandra. This rarely happens in our lives—we have lunch or dinner together most days, and usually spend the night, either at her apartment or my small house. I'm fixing up a house for the two of us, which I don't want her to see until it's finished.

I'd thought proposing to Calandra would let me spend every non-work minute of my life with her, but now I see her less than ever.

Natural, I tell myself. Weddings take up a lot of time. That's why movies are made about weddings, comedies about all the things going wrong.

Another reason is my work—spring is high season for home renovating and building so that the hard labor can be done before the heat hits. I'm also closely supervising work on the new house, rolling up my sleeves and pitching in to connect wiring and plumbing myself.

I don't know if anything's going wrong with our wedding, because I hear little from Calandra. I wonder what she's not telling me. When I try to pry information out of my mom, who is in constant communication with Calandra's mom, she only gives me her *I'm busy* stare.

"Weddings are the woman's prerogative," she tells me when I corner her at the reception desk in our office. "*You* simply need to show up on the day with the ring."

"Not in a sarong," I say adamantly. Austin, who happens to be passing, lets out a snort. "Or a football jersey," I continue loudly. "Or a zoot suit."

"You worry too much." My mother actually pats me, a man of nearly thirty, on the head. "I'll tell you when it's time for your tux fitting."

"I'm not even deciding the tux myself?" I ask in irritation.

"You boys need to match, so I'm setting up the tailor, and you'll show up for the fitting. All right? Now, I've got a mountain of accounting to do, and I'm sure you have clients to talk to."

"I recognize a brush-off when I hear one." I pick up folders from the reception desk, pretending I know what's in them or whether they're even for me.

Our receptionist, Sandra, a woman in her fifties with kindness in her smile but enough steel to put up with us, gives me a sympathetic glance as my mother bustles toward her office.

"Weddings are hell," she says with authority. "I didn't even like my own. But remember, it's not the wedding ceremony that's important. It's what the ceremony represents, your marriage to Calandra."

I huff out a breath. "That's what I keep trying to say."

"Don't fight it. Grit your teeth and bear it. On the other side of the wedding, you'll have Calandra, and she'll have you. In the end, it really doesn't matter if the tuxes don't match or the flowers wilt or the cake falls."

I tap the top of the reception desk with the folders. "You're a wise woman, Sandra."

"I know. Those are Austin's sales data."

"Oh." I lay the folders down. "I think I'll go into my office now and stop making a fool of myself."

"Always best. It will be over before you know it."

"Ha." I say. This has already been the longest month of my life.

———

MORE TIME PASSES, AND I BARELY SEE CALANDRA. Once in a while, we have a break from constant demands to approve the color of the napkins—which changes week to week—or to audition yet another band or taste yet another kind of cake. In these frantic moments, Calandra and I steal away to my house, making love furiously before we're interrupted by more texts and phone calls. *Where are you guys? You need to look at this.*

When I'm not crushed with wedding plans, I work on the house I've bought us, a Mission Revival home in a historic district. I spend a lot of time up to my ears in drywall plaster and plumber's putty, picking out cabinets and fixtures, deciding on paint color while Calandra tries on dress after dress, and the bridesmaids text me pictures.

Calandra looks beautiful in all of them. I say so. Abby's text comes back—*You're no help at all!* Followed by a laughing-until-crying emoji.

What the hell do I know about wedding gowns? Like I say, I barely notice the dress. I see Calandra's smiling, flushed face, her mussed hair, and the sneakers she flashes while grinning at the camera.

I love her so much.

I'll see her on the honeymoon, I tell myself. Except even our honeymoon is hijacked. Plans are being made for me to take Calandra to a tropical getaway on a Caribbean island I'd never heard of, in a huge resort, where people will wait on us hand and foot, and Calandra can spend days at the spa.

Nice of them, but it isn't the kind of place Calandra and I like—no one believes that, by the way. They think we're being polite.

Calandra and I are more outdoorsy, liking overnight hikes to out-of-the-way places in the countryside. We've seen beautiful slot canyons and hiked through parts of the Grand Canyon most people never go. We like to *do* stuff, not sit still and be pampered. I try to explain this to Brooke and Abby, but they stare at me like I'm crazy and don't understand what Calandra wants at all.

Things come to a head when Calandra calls me at midnight on a Friday late in March, just as I'm settling into bed for some peace and quiet.

"Ryan." Her voice is hard, as though she's gritting her teeth to keep from crying. "Get me out of here. *Please.*" I hear her mom and cousins behind her, and know she's been trapped at the family house.

I take two seconds to figure out what to do. I'm all about the grand gesture, and I know one is called for right now.

"Sure thing, baby. Sneak out and meet me in front. I'll be right there."

I make a few phone calls, and I'm gone.

Chapter Four

Calandra

HEY, CALANDRA, WHERE'RE YOU GOING?"
Mandy calls to me as I surreptitiously exit the living
room.

"Thirsty," I say, turning my steps to the kitchen. I
can leave through the back door there and circle
around the house to meet Ryan.

"Me too. I'll join you."

To my consternation, she follows me. I do like my
cousins, who are fun and spontaneous, but if Mandy
sees Ryan show up, he'll be dragged inside and
subjected to more interrogation and teasing about the
wedding, me, our wedding night, you name it. We'll
never get out of here.

I open the refrigerator and take out a bottle of

white wine. I'll pour Mandy a glass and send her off, lingering as though deciding what I want.

Mandy ignores the glass. "It's a little late for wine. I know—let's make margaritas."

I try not to groan. Mandy and her sister have been coming and going from our house in the last month, so she's learned where everything is in the kitchen. She slides out the blender and opens the liquor cabinet to bring out tequila. I'm instructed to find limes and salt.

I produce half a dozen limes from my mom's well-stocked produce drawer and thump a salt grater on the counter.

"You get started," I say. "I need to visit the lady's."

The oldest trick in the book. Mandy nods as she starts dumping ice into the blender, and I hurry through the crowded living room and down the hall to the bedroom wing. I turn on the light in the bathroom then glance over my shoulder.

No one is watching, so I close the bathroom door without going in and tiptoe past it to my parents' bedroom. Thankfully, it's empty—Mom and Dad still going strong with the guests—and I quietly unlock their patio door.

"Calandra?" Mom's voice drifts down the hall. "Honey, you need to come see this. Calandra?"

I swallow my breath and try not to cough. I can either slither out to the patio and make a run for it, or hurry back down the hall and bang open the bathroom door like I've just finished my business.

"She's taking a pee break," Brooke says, laughter in her voice. "Has to with all this wine flowing."

"I'm making margaritas," Mandy yells from the kitchen. The blender whirs.

Under cover of the blender's sound, I slide open the glass door in my parents' bedroom, and put a foot on the patio. I get tangled up in the vertical blinds, which dance around with a muffled jangle, slapping me on the butt.

"Calandra?" My mother's call comes again. "You all right in there?"

Laughter from my friends. More blender whirring. I manage to step over the threshold without tripping, close the door as quietly as possible, and zip toward the dark edge of the patio.

The living room patio door rushes open. "It's so nice out," Candy's voice sings. "We should look at the stars."

"Not if we're having margaritas." Abby's laughter drifts to me as she steps outside. "They'll all look like double stars."

She chuckles, turns her head, and sees me.

We share a long glance, Abby standing under the soft porch lights, poised and pretty, as always. I'm half crouched in the flower bed at the end of the patio, like a wild rabbit trying to keep its distance.

Abby has been my best friend for years. Though she moved across town right before high school, we kept in touch, going to each other's school dances and having sleepovers, and continued to be close. Abby knows me better than anyone.

She gazes at me a moment, then we hear the sound of a pickup purring to a stop on the other side of the back gate.

Abby opens her mouth to call out. Then she shuts it, makes a shooing motion, and turns back to the living room. "It's a little breezy," she says loudly. "Let's stay inside."

I let out a long breath of relief. *I owe you one, my best friend.*

I rise from my hiding place and hurry through the gate, opening and closing it very carefully so it doesn't squeak.

Ryan's pickup waits in front of the house next door. I'm wilting in relief as I run toward it, glad I wore my sturdy sneakers.

Before Ryan can get out to assist me, I wrench open the passenger door and dive in, as though I'm fleeing the scene of a crime.

"Go, go, go!" I yell.

Ryan laughs his fine, rumbling laugh and pulls from the curb slowly so he won't draw attention.

Not until we've turned to a busier street do I ease myself out of the ball I've curled into and look around. We're on Camelback, heading in the direction of my apartment.

"I can't go home," I protest. "They'll search for me at my place. They'll be texting any minute now."

"We're only going there so you can pick up what you need. Then we're outta here."

"We are?" I gaze at Ryan in bewilderment, and then I'm caught by the sight of his strong jaw, dark hair that never lays straight, his arms in a short-sleeved shirt, muscles bunching as he rests his hands lightly on the wheel. I swallow and pull my mind back to the present situation. "Where are we going?"

"On a pre-honeymoon," Ryan says. "I'd already set up a getaway for us if things got bad, and it sounds like they're bad. This weekend is going to be all about the two of us, no texting from our families, no phone calls."

Immediately, my phone buzzes. It's Mandy, wondering where I am and if I'm okay.

"You did?" I stare at Ryan in admiration. I knew I loved him for a reason.

"Yep. Our wedding isn't ours, and our honeymoon won't be ours, but if you take all that away, there's still us. The most important component of this equation."

I rub my arms to keep from launching myself at him and hugging him hard. "You sweetheart, you."

Ryan flashes me the smile that makes me melt every time. "I'm king of the grand gesture, love. And this is my grand gesture. Calandra Stevenson, this weekend is for *you*."

I laugh, relaxing for the first time in a long while. "I'm not even going to ask where you're taking me. I'm gonna sit back, relax, and enjoy my trip."

Ryan has done this before—swept me away to a

weekend of fun, adventure, and great times in bed. He takes me somewhere with incredible wild beauty or to a quiet house on the ocean, or if we stay in a city, a room with a view and a do-not-disturb sign.

I tingle in anticipation.

"Was it that bad?" he asks as we drive through the dark to my apartment. I live fifteen minutes from my mom and dad's house, and tonight, that's way too close.

"I can't remember who brought up our wedding vows," I tell him. "All the sudden, a marriage counselor is going to help us write them so we say the right words to cement a healthy relationship." I drop my head into my hands. "I thought it was a drunk suggestion, a joke, but then Brooke is noting a reminder on Abby's tablet to research marriage counselors. This is after they changed the wedding cake for the tenth time. Now it's five tiers carved to look like a mountain with the bride and groom climbing it."

Ryan's laughter fills the pickup's cab. "Your friends are nuts."

"That suggestion came from your mom. She's there tonight."

His amusement dies. "Is she?" The truck speeds up. "Time to get out of town."

At my apartment, I grab a soft overnight bag from the closet and start throwing things in—underwear, toothbrush, socks, jeans, shorts, and I change into a pair of hiking boots. Everything I'd need for a camping trip. I ponder a moment then add a nice dress and sandals.

Ryan might be taking me to a hotel. I don't want to ruin his surprise, but it's hard to pack for the unknown.

He's not raiding the refrigerator for water or snacks, which might mean we're flying somewhere. I add small bottles of shampoo and travel toothpaste.

As we depart, the door next to mine on the landing opens and my neighbor, Elaine, steps out. She's about twenty years older than me, divorced with a grown daughter, and works a lot.

"Where are you two rushing off to in the middle of the night?" she asks. "Eloping?" She grins, her tired face lighting.

"Not yet," Ryan says. "Just some R&R. Do us a favor—if anyone comes looking, we're fine, and we'll see them later."

Elaine eyes us up and down then winks at me. "Gotcha."

"Appreciate it," I say breathlessly.

"Take care, now. You want to make it to your wedding."

"Oh, we'll be there," Ryan vows. "Good night."

"Good night you two. I never saw you." Elaine retreats inside and locks the door. We hear her soft laughter.

Ryan leads the way down the outside stairs, a flood-light glowing yellow in the darkness, to where he's left his truck parked in my designated space. In a few minutes, we're on the road. I'm correct that we'll be taking a plane, because Ryan pulls into an offsite parking lot on Forty-Fourth Street and hails a courtesy shuttle to take us to the main airport.

The airport is surprisingly quiet as we walk through the wide concourse to security. There's only a small line, and we're soon through. I follow Ryan to the gate and see the name of our destination. Reno.

"Reno?" I say as we take a seat to wait for the plane. "A sudden desire to play blackjack? If so, Las Vegas is closer."

Ryan contrives to look mysterious. "I never said Reno was our final stop."

"Hmm. Intriguing."

I truly am curious. Ryan doesn't gamble and he's not into the twenty-four hour party lifestyle, so I doubt we'll be whooping it up in Reno. He'll sometimes go with his brothers to Vegas and have fun at the shows, but he retreats to his room and calls me or sleeps while Zach and Austin hit the bars. Austin grumbles that Ryan's too sensible and dependable, but Ryan's just understated. *I* always have a fine time with him.

The plane arrives and we board. Ryan has booked us first-class seats, the sweetheart. We sip champagne while the rest of the plane loads and have another once we're in the air. Or, I do, but Ryan sticks with water. This signals to me he plans to drive once we land.

An hour and a half after we take off, we're landing at the small airport in Reno. We don't need to wait for luggage as we carried on what little we brought with us. Ryan takes me to the rental car counter, and here we run into our first snag.

"I reserved an SUV," Ryan says to the rental car clerk when the man shoves a contract for a compact sedan over the counter to Ryan.

The clerk types on his computer and shakes his head. "All the SUVs are out. None coming in until Monday. We can't always guarantee you'll get a specific vehicle."

Ryan's annoyed, but he signs the contract. "Doesn't matter. It's wheels to get from A to B."

The car turns out to be very small. The description, *sedan,* is optimistic, but *compact* is on the nose. But we don't have much stuff, so we shove our bags into the trunk and squeeze ourselves into the front seats.

"Now will you tell me where we're going?" I ask brightly.

Dawn is breaking. It's cold, but bracing, a relief after the 90-degree March heatwave that had hit Phoenix.

Ryan grins at me as he starts the car. "Tahoe, baby."

"Oh." I give a little hop of pleasure. Lake Tahoe and surrounding mountains and woods are beautiful. I know Ryan must have booked us into some gorgeous mountain retreat, not a giant hotel and casino.

He drives onto the I-80 and heads out of Reno to Truckee, where he turns south to the California side of the lake. The sun rises, brushing the mountains with pinks, oranges, and purples. It's so beautiful that tears prick my eyes. Ryan always knows exactly what I need.

Ryan had texted our families when we landed to say we were fine but leave us alone, and then we turned off the ringers and put the phones in the bags when we got into the car. Now there was blessed silence and the immensity of the land and the looming Sierras.

We drive up into the mountains, the lake falling away on our left, the sun rising over it. There's snow here at six-thousand plus feet in March. The road is clear, but there's plenty on the ground.

"It's a small resort," Ryan explains. "We have a little cabin right at the foot of several trails. If there's enough snow we can snowshoe, and if not, we can hike. And then have a nice dinner in a restaurant. Just you and me."

He winks at me, and my body heats. It's been a while since we've been truly alone, no hurried love-making in the dark between texts from our families.

A wave of cold hits me, and I shiver. "I didn't bring a coat. Is this thing working?" I toggle the heat, but only a tiny trickle of warm air emerges.

"There's a gear shop near the resort. We'll stop there and buy jackets and things." Ryan shrugs. "It'll be a little colder than we're used to, but we'll get a fire going in the cabin and snuggle up."

I shiver again, but in delight. "Sounds like bliss."

The road winds up and down hills, revealing spectacular views before plunging once more into deep woods. We pass entrances to large resorts, which are open year-round—for skiing in the winter, lake sports in the summer, and pure beauty in all seasons.

The sports supply store in a small town has barely opened for the day when we stop to buy jackets and sweatshirts more appropriate to the climate. When you live in hot country, you get slack about owning coats and heavy clothes.

"Too slushy for snowshoeing," the guy at the counter informs us. He's a big, beefy older man with massively muscled arms. "Too slushy for much hiking either." He shrugs large shoulders. "A couple months from now, hiking will be great."

"This is kind of a last-minute, emergency getaway." Ryan grins. "We'll just enjoy the scenery."

"Supposed to have some snow today," the man says as he rings up our purchases. "If it's powdery enough, might be good for a last run on the slopes or snowshoeing the back country."

He sounds dubious, but I hadn't rushed here so I could snowshoe. I've come to be with Ryan, to enjoy time alone, away from the wedding frenzy.

We thank the man, take our purchases, and head back to the car. I pause a moment to throw back my shoulders and breathe the fresh mountain breeze. Sun brushes my face, the air so clear it's burning.

It's very quiet, ours the only car in the lot. One

SUV passes slowly on the road, then nothing. A crow soars overhead, its throaty *caw* echoing in the silence.

Once we climb into the car, Ryan continues along the main highway, then takes a dirt road that leads straight up a hill. I hang on as the small car bumps and jounces. I hope we don't get stuck, though a walk in these woods, now that we have warmer gear, won't be a bad thing.

The road levels and Ryan pulls to a halt at a closed gate hung between two trees. A sign beside the gate proclaims that *Mountainside Getaway* lies beyond.

However, a hand-printed red sign in the very middle of the gate says in block letters, *Resort Closed*.

"What the hell?" Ryan sets the brake and hauls himself out of the car. He strides to the gate and peers down the road on the other side, which disappears into the woods. "I called them last night. They know we're coming."

He takes out his phone, glares at it, then shakes it. I dig mine from my bag. No signal.

"Damn it," Ryan snarls.

I pry myself from the car and join him at the gate. "I'm sure it will be okay to leave the car here and walk in to see what's wrong."

Ryan nods, but his eyes are tight. He wants this to be the perfect weekend for me, and things are already turning sour.

I slide my hand into his. "It's so beautiful. I don't mind the walk."

Ryan's tension eases as he glances down at me. "It shouldn't be far."

"Let's go, then."

The gate is locked but Ryan helps me climb it then easily scrambles up and over. The road continues its rutted, narrow, and windy way, and we walk it, hand in hand, enjoying the brisk coolness.

About a half mile later, we come upon cottages tucked into the woods, the rushing noise of a creek behind them.

The houses are tiny, with deep porches and large windows, chimneys proclaiming that log fires await inside. A few doors of these charming cabins are open, but I don't see any people within. Or without—or anywhere.

Ryan cups his hands around his mouth. "Anyone home?"

The smallest house has a wide gravel space in front of it for parking, and I assume this is the front office. A few moments after Ryan shouts, a man emerges, cradling a shotgun, but it rests over his arm, not pointed at us. I sidestep behind Ryan, hoping we haven't landed in some weird, stalker horror movie.

"We're closed," the man says.

"We have a reservation," Ryan says. "Are you Jim? I called you last night. Ryan McLaughlin."

"I remember." The man nods. He appears normal enough, in jeans, sweatshirt, and hiking boots. He's older, like the guy at the sporting goods store, but again, in very good shape. "Sorry about this. We had to close. I called you, but the message must not have gone through."

Ryan checks his phone, which is still giving him nothing. "What happened?"

The man scratches his bearded chin. "Bear infestation.

Chapter Five

Calandra

I POP out from behind Ryan. "Sorry—did you say *bear infestation?*"

A slow nod. "Yep. Hazard of living in deep woods. Four or five black bears came down off the mountain, broke into a couple cabins, and tore them apart. Smashed windows, wrecked furniture, made huge nuisances of themselves. Didn't hurt anyone, fortunately. The rangers herded the bears back up the mountain, but I have to close and wait for the insurance company and repairs. I refunded your deposit."

Ryan lets out his breath. Meanwhile I squish myself close to him, scanning the woods for bears that might return and be annoyed we're in their way.

"Are you covered for partying bears?" I ask Jim.

Jim shows his teeth in a small smile. "I am, as a matter of fact. Sorry I can't help you folks."

"It's all right," Ryan assures him, but he's tense again. "Don't worry, sweetie," he says to me. "These mountains are covered with resorts, and there's more at the lake."

"Most are booked up," Jim tells us in his slow way. "It's the weekend, and might be the last time to enjoy the deep snow before summer."

Ryan manages a nonchalant wave. "I'll check around. Sorry this happened to you."

"Oh, well." Jim shrugs. "It's life in the high country. Come back in July—I should be ready by then."

He gives us a wave goodbye, shoulders the gun, saunters into his office, and closes the door.

Ryan won't look at me. "I'm so sorry, baby."

I rub my shoulder against him. "Don't apologize for bears being bears. At least we weren't here when it happened." I look up at him, my head on his chest. "Being with *you* is really what I want."

Ryan relaxes again. We link hands and stroll back down the road to the car, enjoying the walk under the cool sky.

Once we're buckled up, Ryan reverses the car down the hill until he finds a place to turn around. I pull my coat close in the growing cold as the car reaches the main road, and Ryan turns toward the more populated areas.

Jim proves to be right, however. Every resort we try

is booked—the end of spring break, they say. I'm surprised the college crowd has headed to the mountains instead of the ocean for their week off, but apparently they have.

We visit about half a dozen places, then decide to save gas and call, now that we're in a more built-up area and can use our phones. Both Ryan and I contact nearby hotels and resorts and find the same thing. Booked solid, or we can have a tiny room behind the elevators.

Finally Ryan growls and slams his phone down on top of the car. We're in a parking lot of a small grocery store, and the wind has a sharp note.

"I give up. I'm sor—"

"If you apologize one more time, I'm walking back to Reno without you," I say sternly. I hold up my forefinger. "None of this is your fault. It's mine for thinking I can run away and have everything be perfect."

"It's *supposed* to be perfect." Ryan scowls his frustration. "A special time before we face the howling masses again. One glowing night to show you how much I love you."

"Aw." I step next to him and lean into his tall frame. "I love you too."

He slides his arm around me and kisses the top of my head. "You're my best friend," he whispers. "Always have been."

I snuggle into him. "We don't need to stay here. You can give me one fantastic night at home. We'll go to your house, lock the doors, pull down the shades, and shut down our phones. Plant *Keep Out* signs all over your yard if we want to."

Ryan chuckles, warm vibrations beneath my cheek. "You're right. Let's go back. It was nice to get out of the city for a while, anyway."

"Definitely." Gray clouds are blotting out the blue sky, and the wind has turned icy, but the beauty of the sheer mountains covered with velvety green pines make even bad weather picturesque.

We procure hot coffee from the grocer and sip it in the car, and Ryan reveals another treat lined up for me. "We're not going home on an airline," he announces. "I booked a private jet, and we'll have an aerial tour of the Sierras on the way back. Let me see if they'll take us home today instead of tomorrow."

It sounds terrific, but I'm not surprised, the way things are going, when Ryan's face falls in disappointment as he talks to the pilot on his phone. I can hear the man on the other end loud and clear.

"I'm booked solid today, and I'll probably be cancelling half those flights," the pilot tells him. "Weather. Sorry. I'll refund your deposit."

"At least you're getting all your deposits back," I say cheerfully when Ryan hangs up.

Ryan, tight-lipped, starts thumbing through airline apps on his phone, searching for a flight. Not shockingly, on a Saturday at the end of spring break, they're all booked.

Finally, Ryan throws his phone into the back seat, slams both his hands to the ceiling of the car, and lets out a roar. He balls his hands and presses them to his stomach, emitting a softer growl.

Once his anger is depleted, he blows out a breath and turns to me. "Okay," he says, trying to maintain his patience at the world. "How about a road trip?"

———

Ryan

"That will be fun." Calandra's smile is bright, but I know she's trying to comfort me. "We'll pack a lunch and take turns driving. You, me, and the open road."

Calandra is being sweet and understanding, but I hate that everything is going wrong. When she'd called me for help, I'd thought—*Hey, I'll give her one of the best weekends ever. Show her what marriage to big, bad Ryan will be like.*

It will be like shit for her, if the rest of our life is like this.

I try to calm myself. Nothing too terrible has happened—the resort is closed, the weather is deteriorating, and the awesome private flight with champagne and the works won't be happening. But we're safe and whole, and together. Bonus—it's been almost twelve hours since someone texted us with another zany question about the wedding.

Calandra's right about one thing—we do some awesome road trips. We've camped rough in the desert, sharing a sleeping bag and warming each other in the night. Heaven.

I open my mouth to apologize again, but Calandra's eyes take on a steely look, and I shut up. *Don't be sorry. Make the best of it.* My dad says that a lot, and he's a wise man.

"New plan." I twist myself to fish in the back seat for my phone. I've thrown it into a corner and can't quite reach it, and I start flailing. Calandra calmly skims her hand into the back, picks up my phone, and gives it to me.

"New plan," she prompts.

"We drive around the lake and down into Nevada and home. We can spend the night in Las Vegas, eat at a great restaurant, and then drive on to Phoenix in the morning."

Calandra knows I don't like Vegas, but I will find a very nice hotel that isn't too cheesy. One with a suite that has a bathtub for two.

I get lost thinking about Calandra in the bath with me, bubbles floating gently on her skin and glistening in her hair. She'll reach for me and draw me to her for a warm, damp kiss ...

Calandra waves her hand in front of my face. "You in there? It's getting cold."

I start the car and turn on the heater, which feebly puffs to life.

The next call I make is to the rental company in Reno, to tell them I want to take the car to Phoenix. When they hem and haw, my frustration returns. Calandra gently moves the phone from my mouth. "We can drive back to Reno if we have to," she murmurs. "Try to get a flight from there."

I picture us waiting in the airport for hours on standby, maybe having to search for a hotel room if the wait lasts all night and into the next day. We could be home by then if we drive.

The guy on the other end has a solution. All I have to do is pay through the nose, and we're good.

I glance at Calandra, who is waiting, her brown eyes holding warmth and belief in me.

"Fine," I snap at the guy. "You have my credit card already."

"All taken care of, sir," he says smoothly. "Have a nice trip."

I turn off the phone and press it to my forehead.

"Problem solved," Calandra says, buckling her seat-belt. "I'll pay for half. It's only fair."

"No, you will not." I toss the phone in the back again and turn up the heat. "This is *your* special week-end, *my* treat, *me* being a macho badass. So suck it up."

Calandra laughs. We know each other well enough that she'll let it go, for now. Later, she'll do something for me that's equally grandiose. I look forward to finding out what.

I pull out from the grocery store to the main road, just as the first flakes of snow begin to fall.

———

Ryan

AT FIRST, THE DRIVE IS BEAUTIFUL. WE JOIN THE road that follows the lake, which is a roiling gray blue under the lowering sky. The highway is narrow, cars passing us in the other direction so close they'll scrape our doors any second.

The road climbs, becoming ever more sinuous, the view of the lake receding. I have to slow way down because the visibility has dropped, snow blowing across the road. We rise to look down on Emerald Bay, which is gorgeous—or so says Calandra who's snapping pictures. I have both hands on the wheel trying to keep to the tiny strip of lane allotted to me as the road twists in a corkscrew, a drop-off on either side of us.

By the time we're more or less level again, the snowstorm has surged, charging down from the mountains to dump spring snow everywhere.

Of course, my plans to head into South Lake Tahoe for a break and a late lunch go awry because somewhere I take a wrong turn. If I'd had my phone on, and Calandra hadn't dozed off, and the tiny car, which had seen better days, had had GPS, everything would have been fine.

As it is, I'm miles down the road before I realize my mistake. I pass a turnoff to an airport, but it's a very small building, and I don't actually see any planes behind it.

I keep driving. There are small towns up and down these roads, in theory, and I'm confident we'll find someplace to stop.

I'm more miles along and out into wilderness, snow coming down thick, before I decide that's not going to happen. My stomach growls, and I know that when Calandra wakes up, she'll be hungry. The snacks we bought before we started are long gone.

The mountain roads are steep and start to bend again. I have to go at a crawl, the windshield wipers on high, as snow piles up. Not good. Calandra and I both love the wilderness, but that doesn't mean it isn't dangerous.

I can try to turn around and find my way back to the towns around the lake, or I can keep going. The snow will cease when we get out of the mountains and down into the Nevada desert. It can't be far.

I'm wrong about the storm ending. It follows us along the peaks and down into the valleys. I'm exhausted, the daylight is going—I'm driving so slowly that what should be a short-ish trip is taking hours.

I peer at the gas gauge, which is dropping faster

than it should. Did they rent us a car with a leaky tank? That would be just beautiful.

We won't make it much further. I wake up Calandra, who blinks at the snowy trees and gray road. I can barely see a foot in front of the car. If the road blocks up, and we're here with no food or water—it will make a nice survival story in the papers in a few weeks. The wild country out here is no joke.

"I'm trying to find a place," I say. "We need food, rest, and gas."

Calandra nods. We've done this before, during our trips to the middle of nowhere. One of us drives and the other navigates, and the driver doesn't question where he or she is told to go. When the going gets tough, we become an unstoppable team.

Calandra's quiet for a while, scanning the road. She checks her phone, but we're once again a long way from any cell towers.

"There." Calandra points.

I follow where she's indicating. There's a gate on the road, open, that leads to a smaller road. The gate is well maintained, grooves in the snow beyond showing people have recently gone in or come out. There's a sign, half covered with snow.

I halt the car—I don't bother pulling over, because we'll just get stuck in a ditch. *Last Stop Ranch,* the sign says, in pretty blue lettering. I'm hoping it's a small ski hotel, not someone's actual private ranch. Even if the hotel has no rooms to spare, we can rest in the lobby, find something to eat, and maybe wait out the worst of the storm.

I bump onto the road, which takes us around a couple of hairpin turns and ends in a wide clearing. Before us, behind a curtain of snow, is a long, low house with a couple of pickups in parking spaces in front of it, and a motorcycle that's been covered with a tarp. I pull in next to a pickup and kill the engine.

We're five steps from the front door, but the snow is swirling so thickly we can barely see it. I lean across the console to kiss Calandra's cold lips.

"Ready?"

"Yep." She pulls her coat close and slides her phone into her pocket.

"All right," I say. "One, two, three—go!"

We leap from the car at the same time and dash to the door. I turn under the tiny porch and click the remote to lock the car. No idea why, except habit. I'm thinking any would-be thief is sitting in a warm room with hot coffee right now.

I push open the door and usher Calandra inside. The warmth we find is like a wall, taking my breath away.

We're in what looks like a living room. A young man with dark brown hair sits on a sofa reading a newspaper, his booted feet propped on a coffee table. I don't see a reception desk or a check-in area, or a restaurant, just a small wet bar in one corner with cabinets above it. A slot machine sits next to the back door, switched off, its face dark and silent.

Doesn't matter if there's no food here. It's warm, and my hands tingle as they thaw. I'll take any room, and we can sleep—and other things—to take our minds off being hungry.

Calandra's looking around, consternation on her face. "Uh-oh," she mutters.

"What?"

"We're in Nevada."

"I know," I say, puzzled. "We crossed the border a couple miles back."

Calandra pulls me down and whispers into my ear. "I hate to tell you this, but this isn't a *ranch* ranch." She gives me a pointed look. "Know what I mean?"

Chapter Six

Ryan

FOR A MOMENT, I don't understand what Calandra's trying to tell me. I glance around and see a fairly plain sitting area with couches and chairs and a table against the wall with a few newspapers scattered haphazardly on it.

It's the pictures on the walls—one a drawing of a naked woman lying across a giant cigar and a black-and-white photo of another naked woman, her naughty parts covered by the folds of a giant python—that give me a clue.

I'm wondering if it's a real snake in the picture or if they faked it—I hope they faked it—when it dawns on me what Calandra means.

Bordellos are legal in Nevada, at least in certain areas of certain counties. This one is way out of the way between the base of the mountains and ski country. Apart from the two pictures, I don't see anything to indicate the house is anything but a B&B—no disco lights, no raunchy music, no suggestive women in skimpy clothing sidling out to greet the potential customers. All is quiet, except for the howling wind. The guy reading the newspaper doesn't seem to be in any hurry to race into a bedroom and enjoy himself.

"Can I help you folks?"

The woman who enters from the hall is in her forties, in jeans and a sweatshirt, her hair pulled back into a long ponytail. She has a plump face decorated with bright red lipstick and dark eyeshadow, but she doesn't look like a madam to me, not that I've ever met one.

Before I can think of what to say, Calandra answers. "We're lost." She flashes the woman her sweetest smile. "It's snowing so hard we can't see our hands in front of our faces."

"I figured. No other reason for you to come in here." She thinks about it, and shrugs. "Well, maybe no other reason. It takes all sorts. Milo." She turns to the man who hasn't glanced up from his newspaper. "How many times do I have to tell you, no feet on the furniture."

Milo, without ceasing his reading, elevates his boots three inches off the table.

The woman shakes her head at him and turns back to us. "I'm Maggie. You're welcome to sit here and warm yourselves, as long as you like. Won't be getting much business today. This storm is what my dad used to call a humdinger."

"Thank you," Calandra says in relief. She flops down into a chair and pulls out her phone. "Still no service."

"Not in here," Maggie says. "You can pick it up a few places in town."

I take the chair nearest Calandra's, sinking down wearily. "Town?" I ask.

As soon as I hit the soft cushions, my whole body relaxes, and I start to fall asleep. I fight it, but my eyes close on their own.

"It's called Mountain Vista," Maggie says. "A dot on the map. Got a convenience store, gas sometimes, a little motel. We're about two feet from the California state line ..."

Maggie says more, but I hear nothing. Darkness eases over me, and I'm gone.

The next thing I know, I'm waking up to brightness. Not daylight but electric light. Maggie has vanished, and Calandra is reading a book on her phone. Our overnight bags are sitting at her feet, so she or Maggie must have gone out to fetch them. A younger woman has opened the back door, letting in a gust of cold, which is probably what woke me.

I wipe off the saliva that had slid from my mouth while I slept and hope I didn't snore too much.

The young woman carries a paper bag. "I brought

you some food," she says shyly as she hands the bag to Calandra. "Maggie thought you needed something. I'm Cherise."

The young woman has blond hair with dark roots and wears more makeup than Maggie. She has a pretty face that doesn't need makeup, but I'm not about to say that.

"Thank you," Calandra says with gratitude. "I'm Calandra, and this is Ryan. My fiancé."

"Oh, you're getting married?" Cherise is delighted. "That's awesome. Congratulations. You make a cute couple."

Calandra blushes and peeks into the bags. "This looks wonderful. I'm starving." She rummages, making no move to hand the bag to me.

Milo has finished reading his newspaper, but remains on the sofa, his feet now on the floor. "What are you doing out here in a snowstorm then?" he asks with a chuckle. "Scoping out places for your honeymoon?"

"Taking a breather," Calandra answers. She pulls out a plastic box with a sandwich in it plus a bag of chips and a bottle of water before she passes the bag to me. Not the gourmet meal I'd planned for her, but right now anything is appetizing. "Friends and family were driving us crazy plotting our wedding for us. I really mean plotting."

Maggie walks back in, having heard her. "Yeah, I remember my wedding. Things got real complicated real fast, and I ended up crying most of the time. Should have given me a big clue." She flutters her left hand, which lacks a wedding ring. "It didn't work out."

"Well, I think you two will be just fine," Cherise says. She glances at Milo. "Haven't seen you around for a while, Milo."

"Been busy." Milo idly lifts another newspaper. "Working my ass off. First time in forever I've had a break."

I notice how Cherise is looking at him. She has the same expression I've caught on Calandra's face when she's gazing at me like a woman in love, and I know I'm the luckiest man on the planet. I wonder if Milo notices.

I take out a sandwich for myself and say nothing. For a while, we eat, enjoying the luxury of it. The food tastes amazingly good for stale convenience store take-out, but appetite, my dad always says, is the best sauce.

The window behind me is dark, snow smacking against the pane like grains of sand. "You said there's a motel in the town?"

"A crappy one," Maggie tells us. She's busy shutting the drapes and turning on more lights. A neon sign in the outline of a voluptuous woman glows red in the corner.

"Crappy will be fine with me," Calandra says. "I'm so tired, I won't notice."

"Mmm." Maggie wrinkles her nose. "It has rats. Tell you what. You can stay here. I don't have room in the main house, but I have a guesthouse out back that's private, just for me. Big comfortable bed, nice bathroom. You'll get cold between here and there, but it's not bad."

Calandra and I exchange a glance. The last thing I want is to take Calandra to a rat-infested motel, but staying at a bordello is not what I have in mind either.

Calandra shudders. "I think the rats settle it."

"Good." Maggie gives her a nod. "I'll put on fresh sheets and lay out clean towels. You folks rest here for a while. Cherise is cooking, and we'll have some dinner soon."

"You're very kind," Calandra said.

"Not what you expected, right?" Maggie laughs, and Milo and Cherise join in. "Well, it's not like the old days. Business isn't too good anymore. We get tourists who want the experience, and a few regulars, like Milo, but most men are home taking care of their kids. Which is a good thing. If my man had done that, I probably wouldn't be here."

Without waiting for an answer, she departs out the back door, sending in swirls of snow.

"I'm making my nine-alarm chili," Cherise tells us. "Hotter than five-alarm. I hope that's okay with you. I have some cornbread to cool it down, or I can make you bean soup. That's about all we have right now."

"No, don't go to any trouble," Calandra says. "I love a good chili."

Our road trip has turned bizarre, but I'm so tired,

I've stop caring. Calandra, once she finishes her sandwich, droops against me. I think I'm fine anywhere, anytime, as long as she's with me.

————

Calandra

Not long later we're sitting at a dinner table that looks like anyone else's supper table. The dining room walls are painted a soft yellow with flowered curtains of red, blue, and yellow at the window. The table and chairs are golden oak, and cheerful placemats and napkins more or less match the curtains.

Milo helps Cherise with her big pot of chili, which Maggie ladles into our bowls. It smells wonderful, and my stomach rumbles. The sandwich and snacks in the car were a stopgap, and I realize I haven't had a full meal in more than twenty-four hours.

The chili is great. I fan myself and drink water. Ryan bears it manfully, but even he has to take a big gulp of the chilled beer Maggie brings him. Milo grins as he inhales the chili without stopping.

"Where you folks from?" Maggie asks conversationally.

"Phoenix," I tell her.

"Really? Did you come up here because you miss snow?"

"Obviously," Ryan says.

The wind howls in response, sending snow lashing against the outer wall.

"Surprised you made it in that little bitty car," Milo says. "Roads up here need chains in snow, and four-wheel drive is best."

"A series of unfortunate events," Ryan says. "This is supposed to be a romantic weekend."

Milo starts laughing. Cherise smiles at us and tries not to look at Milo.

As the meal progresses, and we start talking like old friends, I realize I miss nights like this. Before Ryan and I became engaged, I could sit at the table with my family or the McLaughlins and talk about anything. Now we can't open our mouths without someone going on about the wedding and the latest complicated, insane idea to make it memorable.

Of course it will be memorable. I'm marrying Ryan.

My family and friends are frustrating the hell out of me, and I feel guilty for wanting to get away from them. I love them, and I know they mean well, but I wish they would *stop*.

"It's tough," Maggie says, and I realize I've started saying all this out loud. "Those closest to us will mess us up faster than anybody."

Both Cherise and Milo nod as though reflecting on their own experiences.

"Tell me about it," Ryan says. "I work in my dad's

business. I get to put up with my obnoxious brothers all day, every day."

"I haven't seen my brothers in a long time," Cherise says sadly. "They're in the military and deployed, far from home."

"I'm sorry," I say. She's so young, in her early twenties, and I wonder what circumstance brought her *here* of all places. Probably she needed the money. She didn't have the wasted look of a drug addict, or the nervousness of an alcoholic. She drank water and coffee with the meal. I told myself she was better off here in a comfortable house with Maggie than selling herself on the streets in Reno or Vegas.

"Why don't you write to them tonight?" Maggie tells Cherise, compassion in her voice. "That always makes you feel better."

Cherise brightens. "Good idea. I'll have something to talk about. Strangers stranded in the storm. The return of Milo. It's been an eventful day."

I open my mouth to make a quip that I was glad our weird trip would help someone, when all the lights go out.

Chapter Seven

Calandra

CHERISE AND I BOTH SHRIEK, and Milo says, "Whoa. Fuse?"

I feel a breath of air as Maggie goes to the window. "No, everything's gone dark. I can usually see the glow from the town. Nothing. I bet a line blew down or broke."

Milo scrapes back his chair. "I'll see if I can get the generator going."

"I think it's busted, but you're welcome to try." More movement around the room and then a flash of flame. Maggie lights candles she takes from a drawer. Ryan and I get up to help, and Cherise disappears into the kitchen.

"Does this happen a lot?" Ryan asks as he observes the rows of votive candles Maggie sets out.

"Yep. Not usually this late in March, but all winter long, it's lights on, lights off. The generator might not be busted, just out of fuel. We use it a lot."

The candles lend a festive air to the room. Ryan and I help light them and place them around the table and on the sideboard. Maggie ducks into the kitchen then she and Cherise return, Maggie with another basket of cornbread and Cherise with a pie.

"Might as well eat these," Maggie says, setting them down.

Milo returns. "No propane. I'll drive into town and see if I can scare some up."

"Finish your supper first," Maggie tells him, in the exact tone my mother uses with me. "Cherise made apple pie."

Ryan rubs his hands together. "Yum."

Milo looks at it and sits down. "Can't say no to that."

Cherise blushes, but pretends not to notice the implied compliment.

"It's like Christmas," I say as we continue eating. The chili gets devoured as does the second round of cornbread. "Ryan's family does chili on Christmas Eve, and my family always goes over. I guess it's a Southwest thing."

"It's a 'my dad' thing," Ryan says. He accepts the hunk of pie Cherise dishes out. "As long as I can remember, Dad has brought out the huge pot and started braising chunks of meat a few days before Christmas. We all help out, but it's his chili."

"Sounds like you have a good family, Ryan," Maggie says. Cherise hands me pie, and then Milo, before she dishes out for Maggie and herself.

"They're great." Ryan shoves pie into his mouth. "So is this," he says around chewing.

The pie is wonderful, all cinnamon-y and apple-y, with enough sugar for sweetness but not too much. Cherise smiles when I tell her so.

"She's always wanted to be a cook," Maggie says. "Don't signal me to hush, Cherise. They're not going to tell anyone."

"I'm saving to go to cooking school," Cherise says shyly. "Hotels need chefs, and there's plenty of those in Nevada."

Milo chews his pie. "Well, if you make anything this good, I'll go to your restaurant."

Cherise blushes again. Milo is a good-looking young man, and he seems to enjoy Cherise's company. I wonder if they're lovers or he simply comes here to hang out. Maggie might have other girls working here who didn't come in today because of the snow, and Milo could have been waiting for one of them.

I hope not. The romantic in me wants Milo and Cherise to pair off, falling in love and being true to each other.

We finish up the pie. I attempt to help clear the

Give Me One Night 71

table, but Maggie waves me off. I'm a guest and we're tired, she reminds me.

Milo, to my surprise, leaps up to carry dirty dishes into the kitchen. Then he grabs a big coat from a rack in the front room and departs, saying he's off to find the fuel. The residual warmth from the central heating is waning, and Ryan and I fetch our coats as well.

Milo climbs into the big pickup outside and revs it to life. His headlights flash in the windows, then he's gone, inching through the snow toward the road.

Maggie hands Ryan a big lantern flashlight and takes one of her own. We grab our bags and follow her out the back door.

I hunker into my coat and walk close to Ryan, my eyes on the beams of his light and Maggie's. About ten yards behind the house is another low-roofed building, possibly once a garage or carriage house. Maggie unlocks the door and ushers us inside.

We step into a large room with a sofa and chairs in front of a fireplace, and a wide bed behind a screen. Nothing indicates it's on the grounds of a bordello—we might be standing in any well-appointed cabin or B&B, with soft furnishings, a bookcase full of books, a television, and a bathroom, which opens off the bedroom.

"I retreat out here when no one comes," Maggie says. "Kind of my getaway. I'll start up a fire, but it's going to be cold. Though I'm sure you two can find some way to stay warm." She gives us a wink.

Ryan helps Maggie build the fire while I light more

votive candles from the top drawer of the dresser. She's well used to the power outages, apparently.

"How long has Cherise been here?" I ask her conversationally.

"Two years." Maggie hefts a large log onto the grate after the kindling catches. "I met her in Reno, living with a total bastard who was trying to make as much money off her as he could. You know what I mean. Beat her down if she didn't bring home enough. I paid him off and said she could work for me. She reminded me of me at that age, but no one helped *me* out." Maggie grabs another log from Ryan and drops it heavily on the first.

"She has a thing for Milo," I say. "I hope she doesn't get hurt."

"He's a good soul, is Milo, and he likes Cherise fine. I think both of them are too scared to make the first move. I don't mean with sex—they do that plenty."

I cough to hide a laugh, or maybe it's shock that Maggie talks about it so openly. "A relationship in bed and one out of it are different things," I venture.

Ryan shoots me a look, brows high, and Maggie chuckles. "You got that right," she says.

She unfolds to her feet, dusting off her hands. "There. That should at least keep you alive. Come on over in the morning, and have breakfast." Maggie heads for the door, but she turns back at the last minute.

"You two are the real thing," she says. "I can tell. Don't ever doubt that."

She opens and closes the door quickly to keep the cold out. Ryan and I watch through the window as Maggie's light slices across the yard. A smudge of yellower light shows as she opens the door to the main house, and then it's gone.

Ryan closes the curtain.

He comes to me where I've retreated to the middle of the room. I look at him, and he looks at me.

Then Ryan starts to laugh. I join him. In a few seconds, we're hanging on each other, laughing hard. My eyes tear up, but I can't stop.

Ryan holds me, his body warm against mine. Maggie's right. We don't need heat—we just need each other.

We fall onto the bed, landing on our backs, kicking off our wet shoes, and keep on laughing.

"Totally not how I meant this weekend to go," Ryan says, wiping his eyes.

The firelight and candlelight cast wavering shadows over us, and I take his hand. "But we'll remember it."

"Yeah, I'll say we will." Ryan laughs again, the deep vibrating sound I love.

"What happened to us?" I ask after a time. "We used to be so calm. So together."

Ryan rolls onto his side to gaze down at me. "No we didn't. We broke up about a dozen times over the years, remember? On and off, like Maggie's electricity."

"We weren't really broken up," I say reflectively.

"More in a lull. Anytime we were apart, I couldn't think of anyone but you."

Ryan smooths a lock of hair from my cheek. "I never thought of anyone but *you*." His voice softens. "I'm glad we kept finding each other again."

"Me too. Things were fantastic between us. Then we got engaged. Where did we go wrong?"

A flicker of worry enters Ryan's eyes. "You want to call it off?"

"*No.*" I sit up to face him. "I want to be with you for the rest of my life, Ryan McLaughlin. You *are* my life. But I've been so stressed lately that I'm torn between hammering through it or moving to Tahiti and changing my name."

"Can I come with you?" Ryan asks hopefully. "We can both change our names. How about Ron and Matilda Smith?"

"Matilda?" I raise my brows. "You see me as a Matilda?"

"Okay, how about Zoe Superstar?"

I press my fist to his chest, my humor restored. "You are so silly."

"I feel silly. Must be the apple pie."

"Or the chili," I say. "It was damn good."

"Cherise didn't make it for *us*," Ryan says. "Poor girl. I hope she and Milo hit it off and are happy. Like you and me."

This is another reason I love him. He can look at Cherise and see her for what she really is—a young woman who went the wrong way because of bad circumstances. Not a slut he might have a chance with. Such a thing wouldn't even occur to him.

"I love you," I whisper.

"Of course you do. Because I'm king of the grand gesture, prince of the wonderful weekend. Stick with me, babe. You never know what I'll do next."

"You're a shit." I roll off the bed—reluctantly—but real life is intruding. "I call dibs on the bathroom."

Ryan waves me off. I find a very nicely fitted-out bathroom behind a solid oak door with a clawfoot tub under a shower. Ryan and I take turns, then we bring out the toothbrushes. I'm half asleep but I have to smile as Ryan roams the bathroom, checking out the fixtures and cabinets like the house renovator he is.

We stumble into the bedroom again, which has grown marginally warmer from the fire. Maggie must have a lot of experience building them, because this one is burning nicely.

Ryan pulls me into his arms and kisses me. It's a long, warm kiss, one that holds promise behind his weariness.

"What did she say about us keeping each other warm?" he murmurs.

"Mmm." I nuzzle his chest. "Let me see if I can remember."

I lean into Ryan, letting him hold me up. It's been a strange, frustrating day, but at the end of it, I'm in Ryan's embrace, and that's all that counts.

Ryan kisses the top of my head. "Should we check for webcams?"

I jump, and then giggle. "This is Maggie's private retreat, remember? She wouldn't want cameras in here."

"You know that, even though you've just met her?"

"Yes." I snuggle into him again. I feel safe in this room, and warm. "Maggie seems real, you know what I mean? Sincere. I'd check for cameras in the main house, because some people like that. But this room is about her."

Ryan rumbles his skepticism. "Maybe she lures stranded strangers in here and then posts their antics all over the internet."

"The electricity's out, and I didn't notice any computers. Or wi-fi signals, or phone signals."

"You make a good point. In that case ..."

Ryan kisses me with another kiss of slow promise, while his hands cup my hips. Hot excitement flows down my spine, and I wind my arms around him. I haven't been with Ryan—truly *been* with him—for too long.

We've already shucked our coats, and now Ryan eases the sweatshirt I'd donned at the sporting goods store off over my head. I'm still wearing the shirt I'd left home in, a top with buttons holding it closed at my throat. Ryan's strong fingers undo each button, loosening the fabric. As though he's freeing me from restraints, I feel lighter, liberated.

I start pushing off his sweatshirt, then unbutton the Henley beneath and edge that up too. Beneath this I find the bare, well-muscled chest I love to run my hands over, wiry curls of his hair catching on my fingers.

Ryan kisses me as he skims off my shirt then he unfastens the hook of my bra. I land against him, skin-to-skin, rising into his kiss.

I shiver, yearning for him, but Ryan takes this to mean I'm cold. He breaks the kiss, and I make a sound like a whimper.

"We should get under the covers," he says. "Be embarrassing if they find us frozen on the floor with our shirts off."

"We're not going to freeze. The fire feels good." I stretch, liking the way Ryan's eyes flare as he looks me over. "But yes, bed is a good idea."

"Hold on—be right back." Ryan races into the bathroom.

He's out before I can do more than pull back the covers, and drops a box of condoms on the nightstand. "If we go through all these, I bet Maggie has more." He considers. "They probably glow in the dark."

"Don't even think about asking her." I yank down the sheets, which smell fresh. "Maggie's nice."

"Yep. She's getting my nomination for woman of the year." Ryan takes a moment to unbuckle his belt and slide off his jeans and underwear. I sit cross-legged on the bed to watch the show.

Ryan's a beautiful man. Tall, solid, muscles hard from his outdoors lifestyle and the renovation work he does. He doesn't simply sit in an office—he wades in and helps with the construction when he needs to.

The Arizona sun has bronzed his chest, arms, face, and lower legs, but left his thighs and butt pale. His face is handsome, eyes a deep shade of blue, hair so dark it's almost black. He's always been good-looking. When we were nine, I had to fend off other girls from him.

Ryan drinks me in while I ogle him. "You are so beautiful," he says softly.

I heat all the way through, doesn't matter how much the cold is trying to come inside. I have a crackling fire and Ryan to keep it out.

"So are you." I look him up and down. "Especially in nothing but your socks."

Ryan glances in surprise at the pair of white crew socks stretched over his shins, as though he'd forgotten he was wearing them. "They keep my feet warm."

I reach for him. "*I'll* keep you warm."

Ryan's slow smile spreads across his face. "Hot damn. Here I come."

He launches himself at the bed and lands on his side next to me, one elbow bent to prop his head. Well, that's what he attempts. He miscalculates and rolls directly off the side.

I scramble to the edge and look over to find him on his back on the floor. "You all right?"

Ryan growls. He heaves himself up and onto the bed—more carefully this time—then he rolls me down into the mattress, covering my body with his, and kisses me, stifling my laughter.

———

Ryan

Calandra Stevenson, the sexiest woman in the world, is beneath me, and I want nothing more. Her tongue is in my mouth, she suckling on mine. It makes me hard, and I want to devour her.

I slide my hand between us and open the button of her jeans. She helps me wriggle her out of them, even while she kisses me. Underwear next, and at last, we're bare to each other.

I recall the first time we made love. We were in college, and Calandra had invited me to her room, where she'd be alone all night. We had made out before that, covering many of the bases, but we'd never completed the act, having promised our parents we'd wait until we were at least eighteen.

That night, we'd looked into each other's eyes and known it was a perfect moment—that we'd been born to fall in love.

This is another of those moments. We're far from home, stranded, relying on the hospitality of strangers, cold, uncertain about tomorrow.

But we're together, and right now, nothing can touch us.

Calandra brushes my face with soft fingers. I kiss her lips, the taste of her familiar, but also fresh and exciting. It's never the same with Calandra, each time we make love unique.

Her breasts are cushioned against my chest, she and I fitting so well. She runs her hands down my back, tracing my buttocks. She grips me and smiles into her kiss.

"Aren't you sweet?" I say to her. "I'm thinking what a beautiful moment this is, and you're grabbing my ass."

Her eyes dance with wickedness. "It can be a beautiful moment *while* I grab your ass."

"I love you, Calandra."

She squeezes again. "I love you too. I'm naked in bed with you, so I hope we're in love."

I chuckle. "I don't think the people next door agree the two always go together."

"Oh, I think they agree, deep down."

"Maybe." I kiss her. "All I know is I'm incredibly lucky. All this shit happened today, and you're still with me."

"And I always will be."

Calandra's smiles are gone, her gaze serious, her touch seductive. She lifts herself to me for a long, sensuous kiss.

Any other woman might have given me hell for the

way this trip turned out. Thrown the ring at me and walked away, called a better man to take her home. Instead, Calandra held my hand and assured me that none of it was my fault.

Even though it was. I'd planned this journey down to the last tiny detail, calling around to make sure everything was in place after Calandra asked me to take her away.

However, I hadn't made a backup plan. No contingencies for bear invasions, or weather, or getting lost. Even so, Calandra has stuck with me, laughing like it's a good joke.

I reach for a condom, and Calandra helps me put it on. Then I slide inside her, holding her gaze all the way. Love wraps around us and our wild ride begins.

Chapter Eight

Calandra

RYAN'S MAKING love to me, and he is all I need. I forget about everything but the sensation of him inside me and rise to him with a groan, seeking the joy of the moment.

Kisses brush my face, then Ryan pulls back, his blue eyes intense. His face softens as he studies me, then he slides in once more.

I arch to drive him even deeper, the slow glide of him back and forth reaching that itch that no one else can. My skin prickles with excitement, shivers building deep inside.

I try to pull him closer, my desperation winding into a frenzy. We kiss, Ryan's mouth hot, and I nip his chin, then his shoulder, suckling to leave a mark.

Ryan laughs, his fist hitting the mattress beside me. "You little demon."

"That's me," I gasp. I hang on, wrapping my legs around him as he rides me hard, harder.

Screams leave my mouth, which I try to muffle with a pillow. Ryan lifts the pillow away and kisses me, catching my cries. Waves of wild darkness roll over me, each one stronger than the last until I lose all sense of time and place.

I'm with Ryan, and we're one. All feeling begins and ends with him. My heart pumps madly, and my breath is ragged.

Ryan groans, his hips moving, he pressing me into the bed. I hold on and enjoy every undulation.

We merge, our peaks intertwining. I'm laughing as I hit my highest climax, no sense of anything but Ryan inside me, the two of us floating in the void of space.

"I love you!" I shout. He whispers, "I love you, Calandra. Forever."

I shatter and begin the journey down, down, down, toward the bed and reality, the softness of pillows, and the warmth of Ryan on me.

We land safely together, back on Earth, in the cozy little room in the middle of the mountains in the middle of nowhere. We don't belong here and yet we do, cocooned with each other in this hideaway, where it's the two of us and nothing more.

———

IT'S A GOOD THING RYAN'S BROUGHT A WHOLE BOX of condoms, because after sweet moments of catching our breaths, telling each other how much in love we are, and basking in afterglow, I push him onto his back and climb on top.

Ryan grins up at me as I make love to him. He cups my breasts, tells me how beautiful I am, and lays back to enjoy it.

I'm coming in no time, he holding my wrists and me holding his. Ryan rises on his elbows to drive up into me, and he's coming too, very fast.

We fall to the bed, panting, spent. We hold each other, warming in the radiance of the fire.

Halfway through our third time of lovemaking, the lights pop on.

"Thanks, Milo," we say at the same time, and then we laugh as though it's the most hilarious thing ever.

Ryan reaches to the switch beside the bed and turns the lights off. The glow of candles and firelight fills the room with softness. "Better this way," he says.

Candlelight brushes Ryan's golden brown skin and dances in his eyes. "Agreed," I say with conviction.

We drowse then, the long day and night catching up to us. Warmth permeates the room and the bed, and I sleep.

It's been weeks since I've fallen into such a profound and dark sleep. Our troubles are far away and insignificant. No texts to wake us, no frantic phone calls. No gown fittings or agonizing over shoes or the color of the tablecloths.

None of it is important. I know this for truth when I wake in a nest with Ryan curved around me, his quiet breathing filling the space.

I don't rouse him, because I know he's exhausted and feels terrible for dragging me out here. He'll take the blame and mentally flog himself for not providing me the perfect getaway, but maybe one day he'll understand that this trip is perfect the way it is.

I sleep again, and wake when sunshine fills the room. Ryan blinks his eyes open at the same time I do. "Looks like the storm's over." He gestures to the window where a crack in the curtains lets in a flare of sunlight.

"Looks like."

We make no move to roll out of bed and check. It's so comfortable, so peaceful. I could stay here all day.

Ryan begins to kiss my face, trailing the kisses to my neck and collarbone. Eventually, he slides the blankets down, moving the kisses to my breasts. He suckles one nipple, cascading heat through me.

I run my hands over his hard body and kiss him in return. Our mouths meet, hands dance, another condom goes on, and we're making sweet, deep love one more time.

We doze again afterward then finally decide to get up. We slowly leave the bed and make our way to the bathroom. The clawfoot tub fits two if we stand under the shower, behind the curtain that runs all the way around it. We wash each other, making things interesting and fun, though we splash a lot of water to the floor.

After this, we dry each other off, dry the floor, then pull on clothes from our bags. I choose a sweatshirt with "Ski Tahoe" on it, thankful I'd brought hiking boots for this outing.

Before we leave the room, we straighten up and make the bed, wiping down the bathroom. This isn't a hotel, and Maggie shouldn't have to clean up after us.

Once we're bundled into our coats, Ryan opens the door, and we step out into a dazzling silver world. The tall pines around the guesthouse are covered in snow, and about two feet of white blankets the yard between our hideaway and the long ranch house. Frost coats the window panes, catching the light like diamonds.

"How beautiful," I murmur, then I shiver. "If cold."

"Makes a change," Ryan says, gazing around in pleasure.

He appreciates the beauty of the natural world, something I've always liked about him. He incorporates that appreciation into the houses he renovates, making them both functional and enjoyable. Ryan thinks of himself as an average guy, but he has the eye of an artist.

The cold nips at us, and we cease admiring the outdoors and hurry across to the main house. Ryan knocks on the back door, and I hear Cherise sing out, "It's open!"

Ryan pushes through the door and we're assailed with the scents of frying bacon, maple syrup, and coffee. Our stomachs rumble at the same time.

"Morning, folks." Milo is seated on the sofa, reading a different newspaper, a steaming cup in his hands. "If you want coffee, Cherise will fix you up."

Cherise emerges in time to hear this and hands us the coffee she's carrying. "Already done."

I take a cup, thanking Cherise profusely. I close my eyes and inhale the fragrance, then sip. It's not the best coffee I've ever drunk, but it's hot and served with hospitality.

"Newspapers were delivered?" Ryan asks as Cherise disappears to the kitchen and Milo goes back to reading.

"Drove into town and picked it up," Milo says from behind the paper. "The main roads are starting to be cleared in the Tahoe direction. Not so much east or south. But they'll probably start plowing in Carson City and head this way up the hill."

"In that case." I plop down on a chair and stretch out my legs. "I'll enjoy the coffee."

"You won't be going anywhere in a hurry, that's for sure," Milo says. He doesn't look up from the paper, seemingly happy conversing and reading at the same time. "At least not toward Phoenix."

"No rush." I sip, and Ryan sends me a quizzical

glance. I suppose he thought I'd be racing to the car the moment the snow ceased. "It's comfortable in here, it's cold out there, and it's a long drive home," I tell Ryan.

"You could go to Reno and fly back," Milo suggests.

"We tried." Ryan sinks down next to me. "We can't get on a flight for a few days."

"Roads are tricky around here until they're cleared," Milo says, "if you don't know them well. I'm a local trucker—I deliver goods all over the towns from Tahoe to Reno. More so during ski season, but that's winding down."

"So you had time to come and see Cherise," I say, pretending I'm not interested.

Milo lowers the paper enough to peer at me. "She's a special lady."

"Mmm." I leave it at that. None of my business, right? I'm already planning their wedding in a little chapel in Tahoe, reception under the pines, but like I said, none of my business.

I realize with a jolt that my thoughts are exactly the kind our friends have about us. They want us to be happy, to have a grand celebration to launch our life together.

"We should call home," I say to Ryan. "Let everyone know we're okay." I pull out my phone, but there's still no signal.

"You have to be in town in the right spot to use a cell phone." Milo lifts his paper again. "That's why Maggie has a land line."

Ryan and I give each other a startled glance and then start laughing. We're so used to the cell phones we can't leave home without that a land line has never occurred to us.

"Are the phone lines down?" I ask Milo.

"Nope. And the electricity's back—I turned off the generator around five this morning."

Neither Ryan nor I had noticed, since we'd kept the lights off all night, letting the candles gutter around us.

I duck into the kitchen. Maggie is cooking at the stove, her body gyrating as she stirs eggs in a frying pan, while Cherise sets the table for five. I wave to Cherise and ask Maggie if we can use her phone.

"Of course you can, and no, don't bother trying to pay for it. You need to tell your folks you're all right. Phone's on a table behind the wet bar in the living room."

She swivels to the counter to chop green onions and back to the stove to throw them into the pan with a grind of pepper.

"Can I help?" I ask her.

Cherise, laying down a plate, shakes her head vigorously, as though warning me off.

Maggie doesn't turn around. "No one cooks in my kitchen but me and Cherise. You can help by enjoying your coffee and keeping the men out from underfoot."

"That's the hardest job of all," I say jokingly.

"You got that right." Maggie continues cooking, and I return to Ryan.

Ryan locates the phone tucked under the wet bar's counter, lifts it, and frowns at the buttons. "You know that cell phones have taken over when you can't remember your own brother's number," he says. Milo snorts behind his paper.

Ryan has to check the contacts in his cell phone, then he dials. I hear a click as the phone connects, the buzz of a ring, and then a tired voice. "Hello?" The word is wary. I wonder if the number shows up on the other end as *Last Stop Ranch*.

"Hey, Ben. It's Ryan. Your brother. Remember me?"

———

Ryan

BEN'S RESPONSE COMES SLEEPILY. "BARELY. What's up? It's like the crack of dawn."

"It's eight. I've already been jogging," I grin as I give him the lie. But most days, I do get up early for a run. If you don't go at sunrise most of the year in Phoenix, you fry.

"Good for you," Ben growls. "Did you wake me up to tell me that?"

"No, I woke you to tell you Calandra and I are in California—or, wait, Nevada—right on the border—

and that we're enjoying ourselves and will be back tonight or tomorrow morning."

"So that's where you ran off to." Ben sounds more awake now. "Mom's pretty pissed off."

"For taking a weekend with my fiancé? It's not like when we tried to elope when we were eleven."

Ben huffs. "And how did that work out for you?"

My thoughts travel back in time to that exciting afternoon. A nice security guard at the courthouse had called our parents, and my mom had picked us up. Calandra and I hadn't understood that we had to be of legal age to get married. We'd just thought, once I'd convinced Calandra to get herself hitched to me, it would save us a lot of trouble in the long run if we did it right away. Thinking it through, we were correct.

Mom had sat us down and lectured us about finishing school and marrying when we were older and more responsible. I'd tried to explain that we hadn't planned on giving up school, but we'd decided we should have a license to make our relationship official so anyone trying to come between us would back off. I also remember Mom's struggle to keep from laughing.

"This isn't the same thing," I tell Ben, returning myself to the present. "Can you give Mom and Dad and Calandra's parents the message that we're doing good and having fun?"

"Why'd you call *me*?" Ben asks in annoyance.

"Because I knew you'd give me the least hell. Call

Zach and tell him to pass on the word. He'll jump on it."

"Call him yourself ..."

"What's that?" I make a crackling noise in my throat. "Line's bad. Sorry, Ben, got to go." I hang up. Milo snickers on the other side of the room.

"Let me call my mom," Calandra says, reaching for the phone.

I shake my head, setting the phone in its cradle. "Ben will take care of it. So will Zach."

"She'll be worried."

"I know, but I don't want her to give *you* hell. *I'm* the one who stole you away."

"Really?" Calandra frowns. "I remember me diving head-first into your truck and yelling at you to go, go, go."

I gather her close. "Our families are probably so busy planning our wedding, not to mention our lives, that they barely noticed we've been gone, my mom notwithstanding. She's always pissed off at me for some reason anyway."

Calandra gives me her *seriously?* look, but subsides. We'll have to explain ourselves soon enough, and in the meantime, Ben and Zach will make sure everyone knows we're okay.

"If they're driving you that crazy." Milo lowers his paper. "Why don't you two just elope now? Since you're not eleven anymore?"

Chapter Nine

Ryan

AS SOON AS the words are out there, Calandra and I gaze at each other in sudden eagerness tinged with excitement.

"We could," I say slowly. "Las Vegas is on our way home."

Calandra's eyes are alight, her smile wide. Then her fervor dims and she shakes her head. "No. We can't."

I'm not sure why she's negating the idea. Our families have been putting more pressure on Calandra than they have on me, as it's the bride's big day. The groom just has to show up and not pass out.

Before I can answer, Milo rises smoothly, folding his newspaper. "Why don't you two talk about this?"

He glides out to the kitchen, where I hear Cherise greet him gladly.

I face Calandra. She rests her hands on my chest and looks up at me with her beautiful eyes.

"We shouldn't because they love us," she says. "They're being nuts about this wedding because they want to be a part of you and me."

"It's obvious they want to be a *big* part of it ..."

"Think about it. They've supported us from the beginning, haven't they? My parents and yours, your brothers, Abby and Brooke, even my ditzy cousins. Zach, Ben, and Austin included me in everything with you our whole lives. There wasn't a summer when you weren't in our pool or helping my dad cook out, even when you and I were mad at each other. My dad's always considered you an honorary son."

I kiss her forehead. "When I marry you, I'll be a true one."

"Exactly. When we marry *with* them. Our families are as thrilled about this wedding as we are. I don't want to take that away from them."

I study Calandra a long time, from her sincere expression, to the lock of hair brushing her cheek, to her parted lips that I'd kissed so thoroughly all night and into this morning.

"You're a generous soul, Calandra," I say. "With a big heart."

"The big heart is here." She presses her palm flat against my chest. "The moment I called for help, you charged in and rescued me like a knight in shining armor."

"Driving you to a snowed-in bordello," I remind her. "I'm a master planner."

"Everything about this weekend was you helping me out. Like always. Even the times in our life I've pushed you away, you always came back. The universe somehow brings us together again, because it knows we should be."

I hold her, my heart full. "What is the universe telling us now?" I ask, only half-joking.

She lays her head on my shoulder. "That we needed to be totally off the grid to think about things. To meet people life hasn't been as kind to, so we can appreciate what we have. Loving families, friends who will do anything for us."

Calandra is right—as usual. "Yeah, it would be kind of cheesy to sneak off and leave them out of it, " I say. "They'd be mad at us for a long time. Mad at *me*, because they'd be convinced it was my idea."

"I don't want that." Calandra's arms go around me. "I want our wedding to be a time of happiness, surrounded by people we love. Even if they argue about the color of the napkins."

I tilt Calandra's head up and cover her lips with a kiss. I taste the bite of coffee, overlaid with the sweetness of her.

"All right, we'll go," I concede, kissing her again.

"But we're laying down some ground rules when we make it home. It is *our* wedding."

"As it should be." Calandra's relief is clear.

I kiss her again. "But first—I want some of that breakfast. It smells fantastic."

Calandra's wonderful smile spreads across her face. "I love you, Ryan McLaughlin."

I touch the tip of her nose. "I love *you,* soon-to-be Calandra McLaughlin."

She bathes me in a spectacular kiss then takes my hand and leads me to the kitchen, where warm scents and laughter await.

———

Calandra

WE PACK OUR BAGS AND READY OURSELVES TO leave after a large breakfast of bacon and eggs, waffles and toast. The sun is well up, some of the snow already starting to melt. Another thirty miles will take us out of the mountains, Milo says, down into the warm desert.

"Tell you what," Milo tells us when we return to the main house, ready to go. Cherise hands us a care package of leftover pie and cookies for the trip. "Not all the roads are plowed yet, but I know which ones will be the most passible. I'll drive ahead of you and lead you until you reach the main highways to take you south."

"Thanks, that's nice of you," Ryan says.

"No problem. Cherise." Milo turns to her nonchalantly, but I see the flicker of uneasiness in his eyes. "Want to ride along?"

Pure pleasure flushes her cheeks. "Sure. Why not?" She glances at Maggie, who's standing, arms folded, by the kitchen door. "Unless you need me, Mags?"

"Naw, I'm fine," Maggie answers readily. "I'm happy to sit here with my feet up and keep warm."

Cherise, dressed this morning in jeans and a sweatshirt, with no makeup but a little lipstick, beams her thanks and follows Milo and Ryan out the door.

Maggie watches them go. "I hope those two work things out soon. Cherise is the last of my girls, and Milo's really my only customer. If he takes her away, I can retire."

I glance out the front window to see Milo assisting Cherise into his truck. "I think they'll figure it out. I hope so."

"Me too. They've been mooning around each other for two years. If they don't hurry it up, I'm going to have to put my foot down."

I stifle a laugh. "Sometimes someone on the outside has to nudge things in the right direction. Or the universe does."

Maggie shakes her head. "I don't believe in that universe nonsense. Milo has a good job, and she'll be sweet to him. I'll shove them together if I have to."

I hold out my hand. "Thank you for everything, Maggie. You've been so kind."

Maggie accepts my handshake. "No problem, honey. You and Ryan needed a little time out, I could tell. A night to yourselves to understand exactly what was what." She releases my hand. "You two are good together."

"I think we are." I pause. "Can I give you my number, so we can stay in touch?"

Maggie grins, and her face loses ten years. "Sure thing, honey. And if you're ever up this way, you come back and visit. You know, in a guest capacity, not as customers." She winks, and then laughs when I blush.

Maggie adds my number to her cell phone then she enfolds me in a warm, plump embrace. "You take care of yourself, honey. And Ryan. He's a keeper."

I return the hug. "I've known that all my life."

Maggie walks us out. Ryan and I say our final good-byes to her, climb into the tiny car, and follow Milo and Cherise to the road.

———

Calandra

TODAY'S JOURNEY IS SO MUCH DIFFERENT FROM yesterday's. The sun is shining, I've been with Ryan all night, and I feel loved and cared for. We've met some interesting people I'd like to count as friends, and we're rested and well-fed.

Ryan follows Milo's truck down a steep mountain road that is surprisingly free of snow. We discover why when we reach an intersection at the bottom of the hill —a man on a small snowplow is happily blowing the snow away. Milo waves to him, and we inch past.

The next road is wider and seems to have escaped much of the snow, as it's sheltered by huge trees. By the time we reach the end of this road, the snow has receded.

Milo pulls over and gestures us on. Ryan draws alongside him, and I roll down my window.

Milo raises his voice to be heard over the engine of his rumbling truck. "Keep on straight, then turn left when you get to the bottom of the hill. Another few miles on that road, you'll be out of the mountains and heading for the 95."

"Thank you!" we both call. "Bye Cherise," I add. "You go for your dreams, all right?"

Cherise smiles in a puzzled way but waves good-bye. Milo raises his hand, Ryan passes him, and we're off.

"Well, that was an adventure," I say, settling into the seat.

"We're not home yet," Ryan reminds me.

True. We're in a small, crappy car, and while we gassed up at the convenience store in the tiny town near the ranch, who knows when we'll find gas again?

We have Cherise's snacks and bottled water, but it's a long way home.

Milo's directions prove to be perfect. Once we come out of the woods we're on a steep but straight road. The view is spectacular, the flat high desert of Nevada stretching before us to the next dry mountain range. The contrast between the lush green of these mountains and the white-beige desert floor is breathtaking.

The trees end quickly as we descend, and dryness takes over. The snow on the ground ceases in an abrupt, discernible line, and then it's sunshine and blue sky. Ryan and I wriggle out of our jackets and toss them in the back.

This is the way things should be—Ryan and me, on the open road, seeing the beauty of the world. I scan through the radio until I find a station that doesn't crackle too much. It's a country one, and Ryan and I sing along with song after song.

We find the 95 and turn south, traveling beside a knifelike ridge of mountains and around the expanse of lake at Hawthorne.

It's nearing sunset when we hit Las Vegas. We've made our leisurely way along, stopping from time to time to stretch our legs and switch drivers. I'm at the wheel when we see the lights of the Strip glowing faintly under the evening sky.

"Want to spend the night?" Ryan asks. "We can try

to find a room at a decent hotel. It's Sunday—everyone probably left this morning."

"Doesn't matter to me. I kind of have the hankering to get home."

Ryan brightens. "Sounds good. When you get tired, I'll take over."

We stop in Boulder City to use the restrooms and grab more food and drink. Then it's off across the Colorado River and evermore southward toward Phoenix.

Ryan's driving when we crest the final hill and begin our descent toward the Valley. I'm resting my head on his shoulder, warding off sleep.

The lights of the huge city come up quickly and soon we're swallowed in them. I have the sensation that always comes over me once we're back in familiar streets—that I never really left.

We return the rental car at the airport, fetch Ryan's truck, and he drives us to his house in his quiet neighborhood. It's a small place I've come to know well, and love. He's renovating a house for us to move into after our honeymoon, but he hasn't let me see it yet. I know, based on his own cozy house, that it will be wonderful.

Ryan lets us in through the garage and we mutually collapse onto the sofa, bags falling to the floor.

He covers his face with his hands and groans. "Remind me not to whisk you away for a romantic weekend again."

I grin. "No way. I loved it."

Ryan peeks around his fingers at me. "Really?"

"Of course. New experience. Wild and beautiful country, nothing manicured, interesting people." I lean into him. "Best of all, I got to reconnect with you."

"Reconnecting." He lowers his hands and dances his eyebrows up and down. "Is that what the kids are calling it these days?"

"You know what I mean. We were letting all this wedding crap drift us apart."

"I know." Ryan cradles me against him. "I missed you."

"I missed you too." I let out a little sigh. It's warm and silent here, one lone light on against the darkness. I have the urge to find candles and recreate the warm glow of Maggie's guesthouse. "What do we do now?"

"Hmm. Have sex?" Ryan yawns. "Though I'm kind of beat. Won't be able to go all night like I did last night."

"Doofus." I snuggle up. "I mean about the wedding and our zealous families. What do we do? Tell them to back off? You said you wanted to set some ground rules."

"We let them keep on," Ryan says, to my surprise.

I study his curve of jaw dusted with dark beard. "Are you serious?"

"Sure. We'll give them a few parameters but let them run with it. Then when they've twisted everything into a big, overly complicated mess, we step in and untangle it for them."

I think about that. Think about it some more. I find a warm glow building inside. "Because Brooke and your brothers and my mom and your mom will each try to run with it in their own direction, and things will fall apart."

"Yep. And then we wade through the shards, implement our backup plan, and have ourselves a nice wedding."

I lift myself to kiss his chin. "You are a genius."

"I know. It's why you love me."

I brush my thumb to the corner of his mouth, and Ryan lowers his head to kiss my lips.

"What do we tell them about our adventure?" I ask softly.

"Nothing at all."

I sit up, eyes widening. "Nothing? Not even that we had a great time, being vague on where we went?"

Ryan takes on the impish look I love. "Not a damn thing. Let them wonder." He draws me to him again. "You're right that we needed the time to reconnect. To remember what we mean to each other and realize how blessed we are. But it's none of their business."

"You know that if we maintain radio silence, they'll think we had a big fight. Or that we were on the verge of breaking up for good. Or actually broke up."

Ryan's grin warms his eyes. "So? Let them think what they want. All everyone needs to know is that we're home, and we're ready to get married." He glances across the room at a wall calendar with a photograph of a beautiful historic home on it. "In a few weeks."

I jump. I'd known the date in my head, but the reality of it suddenly strikes me. "Wow. Not much time."

"Nope." Ryan's satisfaction intensifies. "I can't wait."

"Really? You're not getting groom jitters? Hoping someone will rescue you from all this?"

"Definitely not. I'm ready to race you down the aisle, baby." He kisses me. "Not letting you get away."

"I'm not going anywhere," I say softly.

The next kiss is deeper, hotter. "Good."

When we come up for air, I suggest, "We can always play it up a little, this conflict between us they'll invent."

Ryan considers, the corners of his lips twitching. "Might be fun. But don't go overboard, or we *will* be sitting in front of a marriage counselor, wondering how we got there."

"Deal." I offer my hand, and he shakes it. "Also, in a year, how about we go back to Maggie's and see how everyone is doing? Celebrate the anniversary of us ... reconnecting."

"A beautiful idea." Ryan's kiss is warm. "Beautiful like you."

"Beautiful? I'm grubby from a fourteen-hour car ride."

"You are the most beautiful woman on the planet." Ryan's breath tingles through me. "I know this."

"You've seen every woman on the planet, have you?"

"Don't have to."

Ryan knows exactly how to melt me. "I love you."

His voice goes low, a sweet rumble. "I think you know by now that I love you too."

"Bed?" I ask.

"Best idea I've heard all day."

We pry ourselves from the sofa and hobble together, arms around each other, to Ryan's bedroom, to take each other with warm, slow loving.

———

Ryan

"And that's how it was." I finish my truncated explanation the next night about where Calandra and I had disappeared to—leaving out almost all of what happened—and glance around the full living room of my parents' house, where Mom has called a meeting.

When I'd walked into work this morning, exhausted as hell and sore from Calandra and me *not* sleeping as much as we should have, Zach, Austin, and my mom had gaped at me as though they'd never seen me before. Ben, who'd been emerging from his IT cave as I'd entered, quickly retreated.

"What are you doing here?" Zach had demanded of me.

"I work here." I'd flicked my gaze to Mom. "Do I still work here?"

"Yes," she'd said tightly. "But I want to know the whole story."

I recalled what Calandra and I had decided last night and hid a grin. "The whole story is, Calandra and I left town, and Calandra and I came back. Now, I need some coffee."

I'd walked away, leaving the three of them with mouths open, befuddled. Only Sandra, our reception-ist, who is leaving soon to live with her daughter and grandchildren, had given me a quiet smile of under-standing

Now as I stand shoulder-to-shoulder with Calandra in my family's living room, many people gaze back at me—my parents, Calandra's, Zach, Austin, Ben, Brooke, Abby, Great Aunt Mary, Candy and Mandy.

They're silent a moment as they stare at us, then everyone starts babbling at once.

Chapter Ten

Ryan

I WAIT for the hubbub to die down. And wait, and wait. Almost everyone in the room is talking nonstop. Only my dad and Calandra's sit back, letting the others go.

Calandra steps in front of me and whistles through her fingers. The shrill note cuts through the air, and the chatter abruptly ceases.

I lift my hands and bring them down in a calming gesture. "First, Calandra and I want to say we love you guys, and we thank you for everything you've done for us so far."

"But ... ?" My mother begins. "I hear a *but* coming." There's steel in her voice. She's tried to corner me all day, but I'd put her off, mostly by diving into work or pretending I was on the phone with very important clients.

"No buts," Calandra says in her gentle tones. "We want you to carry on with what you're doing."

"With a few criteria," I break in.

My mom folds her arms. "That is a *but*."

"Okay, a bitty one." I indicate a tiny size with my finger and thumb. "This wedding is about Calandra and me. How we've been together forever, how we love each other in spite of all we've gone through." I count off my next points. "The rules are, one) we marry in our church where everyone knows us, and two) we don't have a bizarre theme—no sand or zoot suits or me in a sarong. Other than that." I wave both hands. "Go crazy."

Again they all stare at me, and again, everyone bursts into chatter. Ben gives me a thumbs-up, as does Great Aunt Mary. Sandra, invited to the mob scene, sends me a knowing smile. Austin and Zach are retreating to the edges, Zach to escape the feminine chatter, Austin to distance himself from Brooke.

I turn to Calandra and enfold her in my arms. "Think they'll listen?" I say into her ear.

"Doesn't matter." She nuzzles me. "As long as we're together."

"I can go along with that."

I kiss her, drawing her up into me, until Calandra's on tiptoes, kissing me back with a spark of desire. The noise fades, but I feel the love of our families and friends floating around us, completing us.

Exactly the way it should be.

Epilogue

Ryan

I MARRY CALANDRA, the love of my life, on a fine April day. It turns out to be a simple wedding in our church, Calandra beautiful in white silk. I wear a tux— no sarongs in sight. Zach is my best man, my other brothers the groomsmen, our families in the front pews of the church.

Calandra and I had fun playing up reasons for our impromptu trip to the mountains in these last weeks, driving our friends and family more and more nuts. That's all over now, as we gather for mutual gladness.

I eagerly kiss Calandra when the priest pronounces us husband and wife, savoring the sweetness of her. At that moment, I'm the happiest I've ever been in my life.

As we finish the ceremony and turn to make our

exit, Calandra nudges me. "Zach and Abby," she whispers.

I hate to pry my gaze from Calandra, but I glance at my brother and see what she means. Zach's regarding Abby, the maid of honor, as though he's a thirsty man and she's a fountain of crystal clear water.

"Hmm," I whisper back. "Might be something there."

"I hope so."

Any more words are drowned out by the music that sends us down the aisle and out into the sunlight. We're surrounded by family and love, and my heart is full.

It's even fuller ten months later, when I hold my daughter for the first time. Tara is so beautiful that I want to cry. And I do. I'm not ashamed to say tears fall on her downy head. I'd thought I'd loved Calandra all I could at the wedding and the rest of this year, but I'm wrong. *Now* is the perfect moment.

We miss our first anniversary promise to return to Maggie's by a few months, because, well, new baby. I don't think we slept at all, and Tara was too tiny to travel far.

Once Tara is a robust ten-month-old, we pack up all the baby stuff from our beautiful Mission Revival home with its deep, cool porch and red tile roof, and head to Tahoe. This time, I arrange the private flight long in advance, and the weather is great, the beginning of a bright summer.

We rent a car after landing at a small airport and find our way to a hotel that's practical for traveling with kids. I'd always thought I'd prefer a romantic getaway with Calandra than worrying about milk bottles and our stock of diapers, but I'm wrong again. I hope we have a ton of kids, and take them all over the world.

The next morning, I drive south, finding the road I'd accidentally taken a year and a half ago, while Calandra makes faces at Tara in the back seat. Tara loves to laugh, and she's going gangbusters. She's a happy kid.

I notice the first change when we end up at the gate to Maggie's place. We'd debated a long time about bringing Tara here, but decided that standing outside to say hi will be fine. Tara doesn't have to know what goes on inside the house, and won't even remember this trip.

The sign on the gate says, *Last Stop Ranch, Bed and Breakfast.* The lettering has also changed to cheerful yellow on a blue background, surrounded by sunflowers.

Calandra and I glance at each other. I drive in and around the trees to the parking area in front of the house. That too has changed, smoothed out with spaces indicated with wooden stoppers. The house shows the biggest change—the wooden siding newly varnished, and fresh blue paint on the eaves and the door.

The parking lot is full. I pull into a small space between two SUVs.

Calandra and I exit the car, Calandra lifting out Tara, and me unloading the three large bags of baby stuff. When you have kids, I always say, they should come with a maintenance package included.

The door opens as we approach. A mom herds three small boys outside, who start yelling even as they hit open air. Ignoring us, the boys take off at a run, mom trotting after them, telling them to be careful.

Calandra and I exchange another glance. Calandra forges ahead and catches the door before it closes. More changes—the nude women pictures have vanished, and there's soft furniture, flowers in vases, tables with magazines about the Tahoe area on them.

"Hello, welcome to Last Stop—" The young woman who greets us from a desk leaps to her feet, mouth opening in surprise.

She's Cherise, but transformed. The uncertain young woman with too much makeup for her thin face is in a trim pair of slacks with lacy top, her blonde hair pulled into a bun. Only a little bit of lipstick and eyeshadow adorn her. Not only are her clothes and hair different, but her demeanor is as well. Somewhere during the last year and a half, she's found confidence and poise.

"Oh, it's you," she exclaims in delight. "Ryan and Calandra. And who's *this*?"

Cherise's expression melts into enchantment, which is the magic of baby. Tara coos on cue.

"This is Tara," I say, the pride radiating from me to light up the room. "Our daughter."

"Oh, she's adorable."

Tara obligingly takes Cherise's finger and squeezes it tight—she has a masterful grip. Once Cherise is able to pry herself free, she hurries toward the door that leads to the kitchen.

"Maggie! You'll never guess who's here."

"Of course I can't guess from behind a door." Maggie strides out, looking the same as she had when we'd last seen her. She plants her hands on her hips and surveys us in pleasure. "Well, aren't you a feast for sore eyes? Calandra and Ryan, the perfect couple, and a baby for the final touch. How have you been?"

She advances on us and hugs first Calandra plus baby and then me. Maggie thumps me on the back as she embraces me, as though we're old friends.

Maggie stands back and looks us over. "Seems like everything turned out fine."

"It did." Again, my pride leaks out. I'll blow out the lightbulbs if I'm not careful.

"I thought you were going to retire," Calandra says.

Maggie shakes her head. "I considered it, then I realized I've been in business so long, I wouldn't know what to do with myself if I woke up with nothing to do all day. So I decided to stay in business, just a different business. Keeps me out of trouble."

"You never told us," Calandra says. "Remember? I gave you my number."

Maggie shrugs. "Didn't think you'd be interested, and you've been a little busy." She gazes pointedly at me and Tara. "I've been busy too—running a B&B is a lot of work. But I have Cherise to help me with the guests and the cooking, and Milo to make sure nothing in this old house breaks down. He's good at it, and also at hauling supplies to keep us stocked. No more power failures, even in blizzards."

"Oh." Calandra nonchalantly swings a little to rock Tara. "Milo's still around then?"

"We're together," Cherise bursts out. There's the young woman in love we'd seen before. She waves her left hand, which is adorned by a thin gold band plus another band with a diamond. "We got married last fall."

"Congratulations," Calandra cries, and then she and Cherise are hugging and squealing.

Milo takes that moment to walk in, toolbox at his side. "What in—" He stops, and a grin spreads over his face. "Hey, you two. Welcome back."

"Three," Cherise says as she releases Calandra. "This is Tara. Isn't she the cutest thing?"

I tense, hoping Milo doesn't realize that Cherise is now wanting one of her own and decides to bolt.

I shouldn't have worried. Milo, the taciturn driver who took his R&R at Maggie's bordello, softens like pudding. Again, the magic of baby.

"Well, hello there." Milo pokes Tara's tummy. "Aren't you sweet? Pretty, like your mama."

"Isn't she?" Cherise asks in excitement.

Milo stands close to Cherise. "Congratulations," he says to me. "But get ready to fight me for being proudest papa. We haven't told no one this yet, but Cherise is expecting."

"What?" Maggie's shriek fills the lobby. An older couple hurries in from the hall, blinking at the noise. They see Maggie flying at Cherise to embrace her while Milo stands back sheepishly, and they smile and move on outside.

"Congratulations," Calandra says, getting her hug in when Maggie finally releases Cherise. I wring Milo's hand. He's grinning, knowing he's being a sentimental sap and deciding to enjoy it.

"I can still work ..." Cherise begins to Maggie.

"I won't fire you for starting a family," Maggie says. "But we'll have to find you a bigger place to live. They've been in my guesthouse, while I have a room here," she tells us. "We'll either expand that guest-house, or build a second one."

The conversation continues, many suggestions and comments flying back and forth, Tara occasionally interrupting with one of her loud, animated cries.

I slide my arm around Calandra, including Tara in my caress. "Now we sound like our families did before our wedding."

Calandra laughs. "I guess it's human nature. We want to help those we're fond of to be happy."

I kiss first Calandra and Tara, while Cherise, Milo, and Maggie are still planning. "They helped us," I whisper, indicating the three. "And now I'm the happiest man alive."

"And I'm the happiest woman."

I kiss her softly. Tara says, *"Squeeeeee-ah!"*

Calandra and I fall into laughter, and we both kiss our daughter. Tara always has to have the final word.

————

THANK YOU FOR READING! THIS BOOK BRINGS THE series, which began with *This Changes Everything*, full circle. I hope you enjoyed it!

For more contemporary romance, see my small-town series of full-length novels, *Riding Hard*, beginning with *Adam*. The Campbell brothers, and their rivals, the Mallorys, are stunt riders in very close families in the fictional town of Riverbend, Texas.

Also by Jennifer Ashley

The McLaughlin Brothers

(Contemporary Romance)

This Changes Everything

Why Don't You Stay? ... Forever

Never Say Never

Give Me One Night

Riding Hard

(Contemporary Romance)

Adam

Grant

Carter

Tyler

Ross

Kyle

Ray

Shifters Unbound

Pride Mates

Shifter Made ("Prequel" short story)

The Mackenzies Series
(Historical Romance)

The Madness of Lord Ian Mackenzie

Lady Isabella's Scandalous Marriage

The Many Sins of Lord Cameron

The Duke's Perfect Wife

A Mackenzie Family Christmas: The Perfect Gift

The Seduction of Elliot McBride

The Untamed Mackenzie

The Wicked Deeds of Daniel Mackenzie

Scandal and the Duchess

Rules for a Proper Governess

The Stolen Mackenzie Bride

A Mackenzie Clan Gathering

Alec Mackenzie's Art of Seduction

The Devilish Lord Will

A Rogue Meets a Scandalous Lady

A Mackenzie Yuletide

(in print in A Mackenzie Clan Christmas)

About the Author

New York Times bestselling and award-winning author Jennifer Ashley has written more than 100 published novels and novellas in romance, urban fantasy, mystery, and historical fiction under the names Jennifer Ashley, Allyson James, and Ashley Gardner. Jennifer's books have been translated into more than a dozen languages and have earned starred reviews in *Publisher's Weekly* and *Booklist.* When she isn't writing, Jennifer enjoys playing music (guitar, piano, flute), reading, hiking, and building dollhouse miniatures.

More about Jennifer's books can be found at http://www.jenniferashley.com

To keep up to date on her new releases, join her newsletter here:

http://eepurl.com/47kLL

Made in the USA
Las Vegas, NV
04 November 2022